"Kiss

Michael said huskily.

"I will not. The game is over."

But she did kiss him. She could no more have kept from kissing him than she could have stopped a midair fall from a castle window.

"We came here to explore the ruins, remember?" she said against his lips.

"Oh. Yeah. Right. The ruins. I'm fascinated by ruins." But he wasn't looking at the ruins. He was looking at her. His hand was still on her bare midriff. Tristan might be the expert at smoldering looks and bold kisses, but Mike was no slouch at generating sparks of his own.

The MacNorris men each had their own personal brand of appeal . . . Barry's touch had sent electric tingles rushing through her . . . Tristan had set her ablaze with a single kiss . . . and Mike . . .

Mike was the most dangerous of all.

Because she could fall in love with him.

Dear Reader,

Happy Spring! April 1990 is in full bloom—the crocuses are bursting forth, the trees are beginning to bud and though we have an occasional inclement wind, as Shelley wrote in *Ode to the West Wind*, "O Wind, If Winter comes, can Spring be far behind?"

And in this special month of nature's rebirth, we have some wonderful treats in store for you. Silhouette Romance's DIAMOND JUBILEE is in full swing, and this month discover *Harvey's Missing* by Peggy Webb, a delightful romp about a man, a woman and a lovable dog named Harvey (aka George). Then, in May, love is in the air for heroine Lara MacEuan and her handsome, enigmatic hero, Miles Crane, in *Second Time Lucky* by Victoria Glenn.

The DIAMOND JUBILEE—Silhouette Romance's tenth anniversary celebration—is our way of saying thanks to you, our readers. To symbolize the timelessness of love, as well as the modern gift of the tenth anniversary, we're presenting readers with a DIAMOND JUBILEE Silhouette Romance title each month, penned by one of your favorite Silhouette Romance authors. In the coming months, writers such as Marie Ferrarella, Lucy Gordon, Dixie Browning, Phyllis Halldorson—to name just a few—are writing DIAMOND JUBILEE titles especially for you.

And that's not all! Pepper Adams has written a wonderful trilogy—*Cimarron Stories*—set on the plains of Oklahoma. And Laurie Paige has a heartwarming duo coming up— *Homeward Bound*. Be sure to look for them in late spring/ early summer. Much-loved Diana Palmer also has some special treats in store during the months ahead. . . .

I hope you'll enjoy this book and all of the stories to come. Come home to romance—Silhouette Romance—for always!

Sincerely,

Tara Hughes Gavin
Senior Editor

RENA McKAY

Just You and Me

Silhouette *Romance*

Published by Silhouette Books New York

America's Publisher of Contemporary Romance

To my mother
and our happy memories of Scotland,
and to my husband,
who did the driving.

SILHOUETTE BOOKS
300 E. 42nd St., New York, N.Y. 10017

ISBN: 0-373-08713-6

First Silhouette Books printing April 1990

Printed in the U.S.A.

Books by Rena McKay

Silhouette Romance

Bridal Trap #36
Desert Devil #92
Valley of Broken Hearts #239
The Singing Stone #291
Golden Echo #347
Just You and Me #713

RENA McKAY

currently lives in Oregon, and has long been interested in Scotland. She, her husband and mother recently traveled to Scotland to look up the castle that once belonged to some of her ancestors. In addition to travel and castles, Rena also likes reading, cats and long walks on the beach.

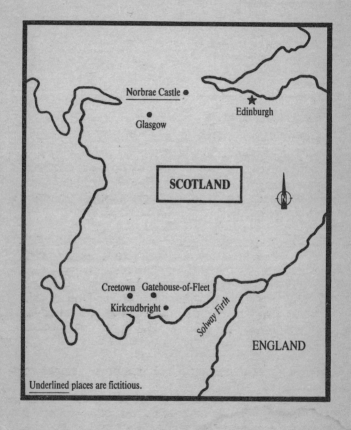

Norbrae Castle ●

● Glasgow

Edinburgh

SCOTLAND

N

Creetown   Gatehouse-of-Fleet
● ●
Kirkcudbright ●

Solway Firth

ENGLAND

Underlined places are fictitious.

Chapter One

Lynn Marquet's gaze followed her roommate's glossy fingernail to the advertisement circled in red.

Scottish castle for rent. Ten bedrooms with fireplaces. Beautiful antiques, trout ponds, heated swimming pool, circular stairways and a dungeon. Come and enjoy superb scenery, fascinating history and luxurious privacy in the Highlands of Scotland. Breakfast, sumptuous dinner and chauffeur-driven Rolls-Royce included in price of $3,000 per day. Contact Baron Conor MacNorris, Norbrae Castle.

An address in Scotland and telephone number completed the ad.

Lynn handed the travel magazine back to her roommate and resumed painting her toenails, one of her regular Saturday morning projects. "So?" she asked.

"So, MacNorris was my mother's maiden name. And Norbrae is the Scottish castle my great-grandfather always told me stories about!"

Melody Corlander swung into a long, slightly breathless account of her family's ancestry. The story went back to some rakish family scandal that had occurred when her great-grandfather was a small boy, after which his line of the family was banished and disinherited.

" 'Aye, and it was a bonny fine place, me lass,' he'd say to me, and he was so sad that he never got to see it again."

"Why don't you write and see if the baron will send you a photograph of the castle?" Lynn suggested. She replaced the cap on the bottle of cinnamon-colored polish and waved a hand over her toenails to encourage faster drying.

"Oh, Lynn, I don't want a photo. I want to *go* there!" Melody pressed the magazine to her chest and twirled dreamily, a halo of blond hair swirling around her shoulders. On someone else the dramatic little spikes of emphasis and vivacious gestures might have come off as phony or overblown, but with Melody they were just an integral part of her bubbly personality. "I think I'm meant to go there! I haven't even thought about the castle in years, and then this magazine practically reached out and grabbed me at the newsstand. It's fate!"

Lynn inspected the magazine again. "Or the fact that they put this gorgeous hunk in a bikini swim suit on the cover," she suggested.

Melody rejected that possibility with an airy wave of one hand, and Lynn had to admit that Melody probably hadn't even noticed the hunk. Melody's regular guy, Lance, who had been trying for months to get her to marry him, was no slouch in the hunk department himself.

"We both have vacations coming in June, and the castle is inviting—no, it's practically *begging* us to come," Melody said. "Can't you feel it?"

Lynn wasn't aware of any mystic tugs, but the idea of vacationing in a Scottish castle was interesting. It would certainly beat last year's vacation, which she had spent with her sister's family at a lake in Minnesota, where the big excitement of the day was seeing who swatted the largest mosquito. However, there was one massive stumbling block.

"We are invited to come, *begged* if you will, providing we have three thousand dollars per day—per *day*—to pay the rent. On that basis, you and I could afford to stay in the castle long enough for one dash up one of the circular stairways, one lap in the heated pool and a hundred foot ride in the Rolls-Royce."

"Oh." Melody plopped down in the nearest chair, her expression crestfallen.

Lynn Marquet and Melody Corlander had shared the apartment for over two years now. Melody was one of the nicest persons Lynn had ever known, good-hearted, kind, bright and generous. She was the most talented and creative employee in the art department at the SunnyDay Greeting Card Company, where Lynn had a considerably less creative job as secretary to the assistant sales manager. But Melody had an adverse relationship with numbers, considered them hostile and subversive, and ignored or avoided them whenever possible.

"I guess I didn't look at the three-thousand-dollar figure," she now admitted unhappily.

"There is one way it might be done," Lynn said thoughtfully. She hated to see Melody disappointed and the idea of a castle vacation *was* intriguing. "We might get a small group of people to go in together and share the expense of renting the castle."

Melody instantly accepted the idea without questions or reservations. "Lynn, that is a terrific idea! Let's do it. I'll bet Kristie Anderson would be interested. She collects antique keys, remember? I know she'd just love to see what she could find in Scotland. And—"

"Wait, slow down," Lynn cautioned. "Let me figure out how many people it would take to make the idea feasible."

She divided three thousand dollars per day by various figures. Six people made an impossible five hundred dollars per person per day. Okay, there were ten bedrooms. Ten people would bring it down to three hundred each per day. Still impossible. But two people could certainly share a room. That would make it a hundred and fifty per day for each person. Still not cheap, especially after adding on airfare, and one week of their two weeks' vacation would be all they could possibly afford. But it wasn't an impossible figure, and this would be a vacation in a castle, not a week in a leaky tent with an air mattress that was always flat by morning. A castle with a resident baron.

An immediate mental picture of the baron flashed into Lynn's mind. A handsome Scot, rugged and independent, perhaps a bit brusque on the surface but sweetly tender underneath. Blue-eyed, fair-complexioned, potently masculine but aristocratically gallant.

Lynn laughed at her brief flash of fantasy. Baron Conor MacNorris was probably almost as ancient as his castle, married to a thrifty Scottish matron, and father or grandfather of a clan of ruddy MacNorris offspring.

Melody was bubbling on about which friends to invite and how much fun they were going to have.

Second thoughts suddenly bombarded Lynn, however, and she wished she'd taken the time to study all angles a bit more thoroughly before mentioning the idea to Melody. First off, two people to a castle bedroom meant a total of twenty people. *Twenty* people, who would all have to co-ordinate vacation dates, travel arrangements and come up with a rather substantial amount of vacation money. They must also be compatible enough to avoid squabbles over who got what room and who got to use the Rolls-Royce at any given time, because twenty people obviously couldn't squeeze into it at once. Twenty *in*compatible people could be a traveling disaster area.

She ran through a mental list of friends. Two or three who might be interested were invariably on the edge of financial ruin and couldn't be depended on to come up with the money. Others had already announced vacation plans or had used up their vacation time during the winter.

Carefully, before Melody could rush in and start packing with impulsive enthusiasm, Lynn made her sit down and listen to the potential roadblocks. Melody was not discouraged.

"If we can't scrape up enough friends who can go, Kristie can do it," she said confidently. "She knows *everyone*. And I'm going to call her right now!"

It was true that Kristie Anderson knew "everyone." Lynn and Melody had met her through some publicity work her public-relations firm had done for SunnyDay, and Kristie was the kind of person who believed in networking and never letting an acquaintance slip into oblivion. Lynn had always thought Kristie's hobby of collecting antique keys a bit odd but harmless. She'd be a valuable ally if the trip to a Scottish castle interested her.

"But even if we round up sufficient people with dollars in hand, the baron might veto the idea of an invasion by twenty young Americans," Lynn warned.

Melody gave her that glowing smile that always captivated both male and female. "You can persuade him. I know you can."

Melody called Kristie, and Kristie stopped by the apartment on her way to a tennis date. She was indeed interested in the trip, but, as she pointed out, neither she nor anyone else could make a definite commitment without knowing a date. She suggested Lynn contact the baron immediately and reserve a week in the first half of June. Lynn hemmed and hawed, reluctant to go that far without at least knowing a few more people were interested. Kristie marched to the phone and within ten minutes had lined up a friend who wrote children's books and was interested in researching a Scottish castle for background material.

"You get a date reserved, and I'll guarantee a full castle," Kristie promised. Tilting her head she added, "For a small discount on my share of the expenses, of course." Kristie was shrewd as well as efficient and capable.

So it was only a few minutes later that Lynn found herself placing a phone call to Scotland. She wasn't certain of the exact time difference between the West Coast of the U.S.A. and Scotland, but she thought it was evening there.

No answer. She tried again ten minutes later. Still no answer. Kristie had to leave for her tennis date then, and Melody had promised to help Lance wax his car. Lynn kept trying the call every ten minutes until she, too, had to leave for a dental appointment.

She was not in a lovely mood when she again tried to call that evening. The numbness in her jaw had worn off, leaving her mouth feeling as if a road-construction crew had been in there working with heavy equipment all day.

This time the phone on the other end was picked up, but for a few moments all she heard were peculiar thrashing and crashing noises, as if the instrument had been dropped in a bucket of crockery. Then there was a muffled "Damn!" and finally a grumpy "Hello."

It was also a very American hello, certainly not what Lynn had expected.

"Perhaps I have the wrong number?" she suggested doubtfully. "I'm trying to call Norbrae Castle in Scotland."

"Lady, it's—" More rustling and crashing noises. "Well, I don't know what time it is because I can't find the clock. But it's the middle of the night. What the hell do you want in the middle of the night?"

Oh, Lord, it *was* the middle of the night in Scotland, and she'd undoubtedly wakened him. She'd earlier thought about the difference in time, but, after her unhappy dental experience, it had completely slipped her mind.

"This is Norbrae Castle?" she asked.

"Yes." The man could make even a single word sound hostile.

"I'm sorry I woke you," Lynn apologized. "I tried to call earlier, but there was no answer. Perhaps I should call at some other time."

"You've already woken me up," he grumbled. "You may as well tell me why you did it."

Lynn was beginning to get a little annoyed with his surly attitude. Okay, she had erred in the timing of her phone call, but this was an establishment that had advertised itself as open for business. If they didn't want to be bothered by international calls at odd hours, they should have put on an answering machine. Her jaw was throbbing again, and she was suddenly out of patience with someone who must be just a bad-tempered underling.

"I'm calling in response to your advertisement about rental of the castle. I may be interested in taking it for a week. The ad indicated that Baron Conor MacNorris should be contacted. To whom am I speaking, please?" Lynn deliberately put enough chill in her voice to frostbite his ear.

She sensed an immediate change in the atmosphere on the other end of the line even before another word came back. When he did speak it was with a new alertness and deference.

"I, uh, that is, we didn't realize the issue of the magazine containing the ad was already out." Another pause before he added, "This is the Baron's secretary."

He was definitely wide awake now, and he apparently realized his sour attitude was not the way to deal with a prospective customer. A customer, Lynn suddenly suspected, he did not want to lose. But the man's changed manner was not enough to placate Lynn's annoyance at having been treated like some unwelcome telephone salesman.

"Perhaps it would be better if I call tomorrow and speak directly with the Baron." Lynn put a little threat in her voice. Let him wonder whether she'd even call again and whether she'd report his bad manners to his employer if she did call.

"That won't be necessary. I can help you. Just let me get my reservations book here—"

"I'd really prefer to speak with the Baron himself at a later time. Perhaps I'll call tomorrow." She went heavy on the "perhaps."

"Well, I . . . uh . . . *Sir?*"

An unintelligible exchange of words followed, after which the male secretary's voice said in a tone of deferential respect, "The Baron will speak with you now."

Small waves of panic fluttered through Lynn. Here she was, a secretary who barely had her secondhand Plymouth paid off, a woman whose family's genetic heritage bore a remarkable resemblance to a "bag of mixed nuts," as her father had once cheerfully put it, and she had just interrupted the sleep of an aristocratic Scottish baron who owned a castle and a Rolls-Royce.

"Hello?" Lynn said tentatively.

The answer came back in a Scottish accent so thick she could barely understand it, but she got out of it that the Baron was apologizing for his secretary's lack of manners. Something about his being a cheeky chap from the States.

"I didn't mean to wake you at such an awkward hour," Lynn said. She felt as if she should call him your honor or something equally respectful, but she didn't know what was proper, so all she said was, "I do apologize."

The Baron accepted the apology and brushed off the late hour as immaterial. He had been reading and was wide awake anyway. Or maybe it was writing. In any case, even though he was difficult to understand, he was full of cheerful good humor, unlike his grumpy secretary. He obviously was a bit elderly to be the handsome Scot of her earlier brief fantasy, but she liked him immediately. She could picture him strolling about the castle grounds in tweeds and cap, hands clasped behind his back, curved pipe in his mouth, dog by his side.

"I saw your advertisement about the castle, and I'm interested in renting it for a week, preferably during the first half of June."

"Jolly good idea. Splendid."

He added some other words that she couldn't quite identify but which apparently indicated hearty approval. He asked where she was calling from and how the weather was. At least, hoping she'd correctly interpreted the thick accent, those were the questions she answered. He said the moors—or was it the mountains?—were still a bit raw there, but June would be a marvelous time for a holiday. He then gave her back to the secretary to take care of the details, adding in a confidential tone, "Verra clever laddie he is, you known, though s'times he has no more tact than would fit on a bumbee's arse."

Lynn thought that an apt statement, and she felt a certain malicious satisfaction as she heard the Baron chastising his secretary for being so ill-mannered to the "lass."

Then the secretary came on the line again. "How may I help you, Miss—?"

"Marquet. Lynn Marquet. And you are...?"

There was a moment's hesitation, as if he'd prefer not to identify himself, but finally he said, "Barry MacNorris."

"I see." Lynn still felt rather frosty toward Barry MacNorris, but she was curious about the same last name. She was also so charmed by the Baron that she even felt a little more kindly toward his grumpy secretary. She might have been ill-tempered, too, if she'd been wakened in the middle of the night. "You're a relative, then?"

"A distant one, from an American branch of the family. I'm just working for the Baron temporarily."

"Well, as I was telling him, I'd like to reserve the castle for a week in the first half of June."

Barry MacNorris was then very polite and helpful. Impoverished relative from the States trying to worm his way into a share of a Scottish inheritance, Lynn decided. It gave her a superior sense of self-confidence in dealing with him.

They settled on the first week in June, and Barry MacNorris then said a ten percent deposit would be required to hold the date. Lynn almost panicked when he named the figure. Making a deposit was so *committed* to what, if one had a pessimistic bent, could appear to be a totally hare-brained scheme.

What if they couldn't corral enough people to pay for the week? If they put up the deposit money, over two thousand dollars, and then had to cancel, they'd lose the deposit. And that would mean all she could afford for a vacation would be crackers and water and a sleeping bag in her own living room.

"Are you there, Miss Marquet?" he asked sharply, after what she realized was an overlong silence on her end of the line.

"Yes, of course."

"Is there a problem about the deposit?"

She detected a sudden hint of suspicion in his voice, as if he thought she might be some...American secretary who couldn't actually afford this and was just playing phone games. She felt an invisible flow of power drifting toward him and immediately snatched it back.

"No problem," she assured him with a resolute show of composure. "I was just glancing through my calendar again. To make certain this doesn't conflict with my other plans for the Riviera and Martinique."

That wasn't a total fabrication, although it came uncomfortably close. She did plan to see France and Martinique someday, hopefully in this lifetime if not necessarily in this decade.

"I'll have a check in the mail to you on Monday. To whom should I make it out?"

"To the Baron. And if you'll notify me of your arrival time, I'll have the chauffeur meet you at the airport."

"Yes, I'll do that. Thank you."

The conversation was over, and she was sitting there tapping the phone with a fingernail before she realized that the question of exactly how many guests would be arriving had not come up.

She debated calling back to discuss this matter. Deep-down she suspected that Barry MacNorris and the baron did not anticipate having a hastily assembled group of twenty young Americans descend on them. Yet the rental rate, and an exorbitant rate it was, she reminded herself, was for the entire castle, and they should expect that if ten bedrooms were advertised, sufficient guests would arrive to fill them. If they were concerned about limiting the number of guests, then it was Barry MacNorris's obligation to make the proper inquiries. With that self-righteous thought to back her up, she skipped a return call.

Lynn, Melody and Kristie each put up a third of the money for the deposit. That made Lynn feel somewhat more confident about all this. If Kristie had her money where her mouth was, she'd definitely round up the people to go along and help pay. The deposit check was in the mail on Monday.

The early recruitment went smoothly enough to further relieve some of Lynn's nervousness. The children's book writer was in, plus a woman from Melody's dance class and a friend of Kristie's who worked for what Kristie said was "the world's stuffiest lawyer."

That, with the original trio of Lynn, Melody and Kristie, made six definite commitments.

It was, however, a long way from twenty, a fact that hung heavily on Lynn's thoughts when several days passed and no more cotravelers were found.

Then Kristie rushed over one evening with good news and a check. "One more down, only thirteen to go!"

Lynn was excited too, until she looked at the check. "But this is from a *man*."

"So?" Kristie asked.

"I know we never discussed exactly what sort of people we'd take along, but I thought—"

"You don't mean you had in mind some all-girl slumber party, do you?" Kristie's mouth fell open in an expression of horrified disbelief. "Lynn, that—that is archaic! Not to mention *sexist*."

Lynn supposed that was true. And yet, adding males somehow gave the expedition a whole different aura. A somewhat racier aura.

"Look, he's an okay guy," Kristie said. "He's an accountant and he always gets me a big refund on my taxes. And time is getting short."

That was also true. And the accountant's check was for his full share of the week's castle rent.

So he was in, and a couple days later so was another single guy. That solved one problem, anyway. They could room together. Then a minor television personality who was a client of Kristie's public-relations firm said she and her boyfriend would like to go together.

Lynn knew there was nothing unusual about that, but again it seemed to put their traveling group on a different footing than she had anticipated. Yet, as Kristie again pointed out, time was getting ever shorter and they couldn't afford to be too fussy. They'd have to make plane reservations soon.

Then the accountant came up with friends who wanted to go, an older married couple who were into genealogy and wanted to check out their Scottish roots. They in turn produced another young married couple, relatives of friends, who were named, a bit confusingly, Chris and Christy.

Inclusion of the married couples made Lynn's prickled nerves relax. They added a sense of respectability to what was beginning to seem like a floating singles party. The married couples could even be considered chaperons.

By the time Lynn invited everyone to the apartment for a pretrip, get-acquainted evening, there were the two married couples, three sets of non-marrieds traveling together as couples, six unattached women and four unattached males. They'd done it, reached the twenty-person quota!

But it was also when some of Lynn's first misgivings dropped on her like a load of SunnyDay greeting cards returning unsold. This was not a comfortable group of old friends who knew each other well. This was a motley assortment of acquaintances, friends of friends and total strangers who knew almost nothing about each other.

The lawyer's secretary, whom Lynn had somehow assumed would be as stuffy as her employer, showed up wearing a slinky bustier made of what looked like—but surely couldn't be—gold snakeskin.

The accountant sidled up to Lynn and said that if she didn't already have a castle roommate, he was available. By the time this man of numbers slunk away under Lynn's withering gaze she felt as if her bust, waist and hip measurements had been calculated and her potential sexual prowess rated on a scale of one to ten.

The male halves of two of the unmarried couples, each of whom hadn't known the other was going on the trip, had once been business partners and were presently embroiled in a bitter legal battle.

Chris and Christy, the younger pair of the married couples whom Lynn had counted on to add a conservative note to the group, turned out to be newlyweds who couldn't keep their hands off each other. The castle trip was going to be their honeymoon. Watching them cavort on her sofa, Lynn thought she might have to slosh a pitcher of ice water over them at any moment.

And the other married couple, Grant and Lily Dunbar, those older folks so interested in their Scottish roots, blithely announced that theirs was an open marriage, that they gave each other "every freedom to seek out fulfilling new relationships." Grant Dunbar inspected the female members of the group as if making a private wish list of relationships he'd like to fulfill.

It was not a gathering to convince Lynn that this had been one of her all-time greatest vacation ideas.

Afterward, an unrelated question rose in her mind. Why hadn't Melody invited Lance along on this trip? She asked Melody about this, but Melody uncharacteristically came up with some evasive jargon about needing "space" away from Lance for a few days.

That seemed odd, since Melody was very much the bubbling extrovert, but Lynn didn't have time to think about that minor matter in the next few days. She had clothes to get cleaned and packing to do and a letter to write to the Baron to notify him of their arrival time.

There were last minute details to take care of at the office with the woman who was temporarily taking her place: showing her the peculiarities of the word processor, what to do if the stapler jammed, and especially making certain she realized the importance of ending every letter with the required company slogan, "Have yourself a SunnyDay." Lynn guiltily realized she'd be happy not to have to write that particular sickeningly sweet phrase for the next two weeks. She'd almost gagged on it when she first started the job, although she'd always kept her opinions to herself, of course. Working at SunnyDay might not be the most gratifying job in the world, but it was secure. And security was something she'd desperately needed after her breakup with Larry.

Fortunately, Kristie had contacts through her public-relations office that enabled the entire group to get reservations on the same flight, an accomplishment Lynn considered both a minor miracle and a good omen. They would leave on Friday evening and fly nonstop to London, where they would change planes for the fifty-five minute flight up to Scotland.

Lynn felt a little dazed as they stood in line to board the plane. It really was happening. They were going to spend a week at a castle in Scotland, with a resident baron and a chauffeured Rolls-Royce.

She felt somewhat less uneasy about her traveling companions than she had the night of the gathering at her apartment. Granted, the married couples hadn't lived up to expectations, and if that accountant made another move on her she was going to give him a jab with her elbow that would have him counting his broken ribs. But most of the others, although they may have a few quirks, were surely basically nice, average people.

And then she saw one of the single men, whose name she couldn't recall at the moment, but who was very clean cut and nice looking, surreptitiously peer into the inside pocket of his expensively styled suit jacket.

He had a rat in there, a plump, wiggly, pink-nosed white rat. Lynn couldn't believe it. Her first inclination was to march over and shout at him in no uncertain terms what she thought of such a ridiculous, juvenile stunt.

But making a scene could backfire, she realized immediately. She was certain that there were strict regulations about taking live creatures into foreign countries, and if the authorities caught someone attempting to smuggle one in there would surely be unpleasant problems. The whole group might be detained and delayed.

Lynn's nerves scrunched into hard knots again.

The thing to do, she decided, was quietly tell Mark—yes, that was his name, Mark—that he must get rid of his illegal baggage *now*, before they boarded the plane.

She squeezed around the children's book writer and the lovey-dovey Chris and Christy, whose arms appeared to have become welded into an interlocked position when they wed. But she was stopped by the strong, straight arm of Grant Dunbar, the open marriage man, who wanted to know whether suits were required in the swimming pool.

And by the time she got over that shock enough to inform him coldly that yes, suits were definitely required, Mark and his rat had disappeared into the plane.

She took a deep breath. It was too late to do anything. She was simply going to pretend she'd never seen what she'd seen and not even wonder *why* a grown man would carry a rat to Scotland in his suit-jacket pocket.

Lynn settled into her seat with Melody on one side and Reva, the children's book writer, on the other. They had a surprisingly good meal and a movie she hadn't seen. Nothing peculiar happened with her group.

The stewardess brought blankets and pillows. Lynn slept, even though Reva kept her light on and scribbled industriously in a steno notebook. It was nice to know that Reva, at least, wasn't going to do anything odd, that she was simply working on another of her stories about furry animals that spouted sage bits of wisdom.

Lynn lost track of hours as they jetted across time zones, but she was hungry when the next meal was served. Everything was going to be fine, she assured herself. The rat was undiscovered, Chris and Christy hadn't been arrested for anything indecent and soon they would be in Scotland where, other than sleeping in the same castle with these people, she could conduct her vacation as if most of them didn't exist.

But it was also during the meal that Lynn happened to glance at some of Reva's scribbles in the open notebook. She practically choked on her roll when she saw what was written there.

Reva noticed the reaction. She smiled, pleased. "Shocking, isn't it? It's all about a group of people stranded in an isolated castle for a week. It has murder and lust and money and ruthless ambition, all the ingredients necessary to hit the bestseller lists. You have no idea how tired I am of writing insipid little stories about sweet little animals for bratty little children," she declared with a self-righteous air.

"Really?" Lynn asked a bit faintly.

Reva tucked the notebook into an open pocket of her purse. "I'm looking forward to doing in-depth research on this trip," she added brightly.

Lynn tried not to consider too closely exactly how murder, lust, money and ruthless ambition might be connected with her vacation.

The pilot made an announcement that London was misty, but the weather prediction was for clearing skies later. They'd be landing in forty-three minutes.

Some five minutes later, Mark leaned across Melody and spoke to Lynn. "May I speak to you privately for a moment? And would you bring your purse?"

Puzzled, Lynn picked up her purse and followed him to an open space near the restrooms. He looked as if he hadn't slept well and he was holding his chest, which alarmed Lynn. Heart attack?

No. Rat attack.

In a hurried whisper he explained that the pet rat he'd brought along had chewed through his pocket, so he had stuffed it inside his shirt, where it was now trying to excavate a den under his armpit. Even as he spoke Lynn could see a lump squirming in that area.

"What could possibly have possessed you to bring a rat with you?" she hissed in exasperation.

"No one would keep him, and I couldn't leave him alone in my apartment." Mark sounded slightly offended that his virtuous motives had come under attack. "I have a folding cage in my luggage. He'll be no trouble once we get to the castle. Anyway, let me see your purse—"

Stupidly, Lynn held up her purse. He unzipped a compartment and peered inside.

"That's great. Terrific. Nice and roomy."

And before Lynn realized what he had in mind he had grabbed the rat and stuffed it into her purse.

"His name is Spike," he whispered. "Thanks a lot." Mark beamed appreciatively, as if all this were something she had *offered* to do. He gave the approaching stewardess a big, innocent smile and asked for a cup of tea.

And left Lynn standing there with a rat named Spike in her purse.

Well, she was not going to try to sneak an illegal rat into a foreign country. She would simply turn it loose in the restroom and let the stewardess take care of the situation when it was discovered. The rat was not her responsibility.

She stepped briskly into the restroom, locked the door and opened the compartment of her purse. The rat looked out at her with bright eyes and wiggly nose. He put a foot trustingly on her finger.

Oh, damn. Dismay and frustration surged through her. She'd always been a sucker for small animals, even rats. She'd had one as a pet when she was a little girl.

She looked around the tiny room. If she abandoned the rat in here, he might crawl into the waste paper slot and get bundled off with the trash. Or maybe some clod-footed man would discover and stomp him. Or—

She muttered an unladylike oath under her breath, gave the rat the crumbled remains of a wrapped cracker and re-zipped the compartment, leaving a tiny opening for air. The rat apparently didn't show up on airport detection machines, so maybe she could make it through with him. It was not as if she were trying to smuggle in drugs or a dangerous weapon, she reminded herself. It was just an innocent little pet rat. They couldn't do any more than confiscate Spike even if they discovered him.

Unless the authorities suspected a drug-stuffed rat was some devious new way to sneak illegal contraband into the country.

They landed and got past the various British authorities without incident, other than that Lynn produced enough nervous perspiration to rival the London mist. Which, despite the pilot's cheery predictions, had turned to pouring rain.

Everyone seemed a bit dazed by the long trip, and they boarded the smaller plane docilely. But unfortunately, at least from Lynn's point of view, spirits revived during the short flight up to Scotland. The unattached males were the biggest offenders.

They indulged in ostentatious flirting with the stewardesses, including invitations to "come up and see us at the castle." There were raucous jokes and an awful rendition of a song about the bonny, bonny banks of Loch Lomond.

Maybe back home these people, some of them, anyway, were ordinary, normal people, Lynn thought grimly, but apparently there was something about being on vacation far from their native land that lowered their inhibitions. They were behaving in ways they would never dream of behaving at their offices or clubs.

This could be, she thought bleakly, a long, *long* week.

Lynn didn't know how she was supposed to recognize the chauffeur when they arrived at the Glasgow airport, but they were such an obvious group of Americans that she assumed he would present himself to them.

He did. She heard Melody's small gasp of delight and turned to find a handsome Scot striding toward them. Rough blond hair and mustache—and a kilt! Muscular legs, shoulders broad enough to inspire heroic poetry, confident stride. Jaunty tam atop the blond curls, spectacular blue eyes, dark plaid skirt, even an authentic *sgian dubh*, that wicked little Scottish knife, tucked in the top of his thick, knee-high socks.

If Lynn had ever doubted a man could be masculine in a skirt, she doubted it no more. He wore it with a confident swagger and a sizzling sexual energy. He was magnificent.

Chapter Two

Is that the baron?'' Melody whispered.

For a moment Lynn thought it must be, that the baron himself had decided to meet them and the chauffeur was waiting outside with the Rolls-Royce. But on second thought she realized this good-looking guy was much too young to be the man she had spoken to on the phone. His mouth beneath the rugged blond mustache was tight-lipped as he inspected the large group of Americans milling around.

Lynn stepped forward. "I'm Lynn Marquet. Are you from Norbrae?"

If it weren't for the fact that she could see no reason for it, she would have thought the expression in his blue eyes registered surprise. His openly appraising gaze took in her hazel eyes and shoulder-length brown hair, and then flowed boldly over the curves of her leggy figure in a white blouse and black pants. The visual stroke went beyond the bounds of polite society, especially when it actually came to a momentary halt on her breasts. She was about to make some cutting remark to show him what she thought of this unexpected treatment, but when his eyes jerked back up to meet hers there was a faint scowl of disapproval on his face. She hadn't expected that, and it threw her off balance.

He nodded. "Aye, I'm the chauffeur from Norbrae."

On second thought, she suspected she knew exactly why he was surprised that she was Lynn Marquet, and she also suspected the disapproval had nothing to do with what he saw. Barry MacNorris had probably told him to be on the lookout for an ill-tempered, sour-faced American witch temporarily riding a jet instead of her broomstick.

She was suddenly determined to dispel that unfair advance publicity. She put on her warmest smile and held out her hand. "We're really looking forward to our week at the castle."

He shook hands with her, his grip not hard enough to be painful but firm enough to let her know that he could bring her to her knees if he wanted to. He looked over her head at the group.

"Are all these . . . lads and lassies with you?"

Melody stepped up. If Lynn had ever seen anyone smitten at first sight, it was Melody. "I am," she breathed. A cartoonist would have drawn her eyes as stars.

Melody's totally unexpected reaction to the man surprised Lynn. Even more surprising was the sharp stab of dismay that reaction sent through her. Odd as it might seem, she and Melody had never been attracted to the same man. Not that she was really *attracted* to this man, Lynn assured herself. Not with that outrageous measuring-her-for-my-bed appraisal he'd given her. But he was incredibly physically attractive—in a blatant, superstud sort of way, of course.

It had been a long time since she'd been so aware of a man; as if a kind of free-flowing electricity jazzed her nerves when he spoke or looked at her. It was disconcerting. She hadn't sworn off men since her divorce from Larry three years ago. She dated fairly often and usually enjoyed herself, but she'd never been wildly attracted to any man. Most of the men she met struck her the same way that a popular tourist spot would—a nice place to visit but she wouldn't want to live there.

Lynn was suddenly aware of certain noises, snickers actually, behind her. And she was just as suddenly furious. Those idiot males they had foolishly let come along were finding some sort of stupid amusement in a man wearing a skirt. *They* should look half as good, she thought, angry and humiliated at this incredible boorishness.

The chauffeur did not appear to notice the fraternity party atmosphere, however. He was just looking at the size of the milling group.

"I nae believe the baron was expectin' quite so many," he observed, jaw tight as a steel trap.

The last thing Lynn wanted was to get into an argument with him, which would no doubt only reinforce whatever unflattering remarks Barry MacNorris had made about her. Carefully she said she would discuss the castle arrangements with the baron or his secretary later.

"I realize that we won't all be able to fit into the Rolls-Royce, but some of us can wait here for you to make a second trip," she added.

Behind her she heard more snickers, and then poorly concealed whispers about the point she should have known would arouse the curiosity of this traveling clown show. What, if anything, was he wearing under the kilt?

She thought he must have heard, too, but again no reaction.

"The Rolls-Royce is in the shop, I'm verra sorry to say, and the other transp'shun is a wee bit smaller."

"I see. Well, whatever it is, let's be on our way."

As he turned smartly on his heel the skirt swirled about his legs, causing a few more snickers. He suddenly stopped short and turned to face the group. His blue eyes glittered steel-and-glass splinters as his gaze moved slowly from person to person, sparing neither male nor female. The look he planted on Lynn appeared particularly hostile, which seemed unfair since she had been neither snickering nor whispering.

"If any of you lads or lassies have in your wee minds investigatin' what is under me kilt, be warned ye'll pull back a bloody stump if you try to take a peek."

He smiled grimly, folded his arms and tilted his head as if he might welcome a peek so he could carry out his threat. The only reaction from the group, however, was an astonished silence. The men had apparently suddenly become aware of the lean and powerful body under that kilt and the clenched fists, and there was no mistaking the poised menace of those words, even though they were spoken in the polite voice of a young man greeting his best girl's parents.

He waited a moment more, spread-legged stance still challenging, until, apparently satisfied with the stunned looks he saw, he turned to lead the way again. The skirt swirled almost flamboyantly about his legs, but this time there was not so much as a trace of snicker or whisper.

In fact, everyone was so intimidated by the unexpected show of leashed temper that there were no more than a few barely audible murmurs of disappointment when they reached the substitute vehicle. It and a Rolls-Royce might both come under the generic term automobile, but there the similarity ended.

"It is *small*, isn't it?" Lynn said. It was some foreign make she'd never heard of, somewhat worse for wear, and appeared made for a maximum of four or five people. She figured with some lapsitting and breath holding they might squeeze in six or seven at most.

The chauffeur didn't seem inclined to offer suggestions. He simply stood there, muscular legs spread, arms folded, gaze focused somewhere over their heads. He looked, Lynn thought, as if he was quite capable of standing there ignoring them until they melted away in the drizzling rain.

"Well, hey, look," Bill Myerson, the accountant, said, "why don't two or three of us just rent cars? We're probably going to need some extras even when the Rolls-Royce gets out of the shop because we won't all want to go to the same places.''

Lynn looked at the accountant gratefully, experiencing the first kind feelings she'd had for him.

He, Kristie and the open marriage couple went inside to arrange for rental cars. The others also scurried back inside the shelter of the terminal building. Melody kept looking at the chauffeur as if she'd like to ride off into a sunset with him—if there were a sunset somewhere in all this rain.

''What's your name?'' Melody asked finally. She, more petite than Lynn, had to look far up at him. She looked delicately lovely, vulnerable and completely thunderstruck. Lynn felt an unexpected and unladylike urge to kick her in the shins and remind her of faithful Lance waiting back home.

''This is my roommate, Melody Corlander,'' Lynn said to the chauffeur, although, considering the way they were looking at each other, introductions almost seemed superfluous.

''I'm Tristan.'' He addressed Melody, favoring her with a dazzling smile and ignoring Lynn with what appeared a deliberate rudeness.

Melody breathed the name as if it were some magic incantation, but Lynn asked, ''Tristan what?''

''MacNorris.'' He rolled the rs in such a heavy Scottish burr that the name came out sounding much longer than it actually was.

Somehow Lynn wasn't surprised. That marvelously cheerful old baron probably had a thrifty Scots streak and shrewdly took advantage of all the younger MacNorrises who had a hopeful eye on the castle and title.

''So am I,'' Melody said. ''A MacNorris, that is.''

In rather breathless tones Melody explained that her mother's maiden name had been MacNorris. She told him the family tale of scandal and banishment. He'd apparently never heard it before. His blue eyes stayed on her, his expression attentive and warm, and Lynn was annoyed with herself for feeling a flicker of envy. She was curious about his relationship to the baron but didn't feel she should come right out and ask personal, nosy questions. Melody, however, had no such inhibitions.

"Are you married?" Melody asked.

It was a blunt question on short acquaintance, but Melody could get away with things like that. Tristan didn't seem to mind at all.

"Not even spoken fer," he assured her, and the smile he bestowed on her was again much different than the steel-eyed flash he'd given the group as a whole, and Lynn in particular.

The rental cars arrived, also on the small side, and even with four vehicles there was barely room to squeeze in all the people and luggage. Melody, who obviously didn't care that there was no Rolls-Royce so long as there was a Tristan, unhesitatingly outmaneuvered Reva for a seat next to Tristan in the castle car. Lynn, feeling responsible for seeing that all guests and their luggage were properly accounted for, got stuck in the last car, with the accountant driving. Mark was in the back seat, and this did give her the opportunity to dump Spike in his lap, to the accompaniment of surprised shrieks from the other woman in the back seat.

Lynn ignored the commotion. Let Mark explain his rat, if he could. She simply warned, "You'd better figure out some different arrangements for the return flight, because I am not going to be your rat runner."

Then she turned her attention to the countryside, only minimally distracted by Bill Myerson's jerky first efforts at British-style driving. Rain still veiled the hills, but everything was wonderfully green. Picturesque stone walls, banked with masses of golden-blossomed Scotch broom and purple rhododendron, lined the roads, and here and there fairy-tale castles peeked out from among the mist-draped hills and trees.

And Norbrae was surely the most fairy-tale of them all. It was not small by any means, but in comparison with some of the towering, sprawling structures they had seen it appeared almost miniature. A magical profusion of towers and turrets sprouted from it. The long, narrow lower windows were deeply recessed into thick stone walls, and the tiny upper windows looked made to frame a romantic princess watching for her knight. The castle projected an aura of timeless dignity, but at the same time it was so perfect that it seemed not quite real.

Exquisite, Lynn breathed to herself as she got out of the car. Melody was already standing with hands clasped, looking up at the castle, unmindful of the falling rain. Two white swans floated on a tiny lake nearby, also so perfect that until one gracefully stretched its long neck they, too, looked more like decorations in a dream than real life.

Others were also oohing and aahing over the castle. Not so the car drivers, who were comparing notes on how difficult it was to drive on the wrong side of the road, with the steering wheel on the wrong side of the car and the gearshift on the wrong side of the steering wheel. Lynn thought about pointing out to them that *different* wasn't necessarily *wrong*, but she figured that with this bunch it would be a waste of breath.

Lynn had hoped the baron would meet them, but neither he nor the male secretary was anywhere in sight. Tristan helped carry luggage inside, where a Scottish woman with red hair, a wonderfully quaint accent and the loveliest complexion Lynn had ever seen, welcomed them.

While the woman was showing people to their bedrooms, Lynn spoke with Tristan about contacting the secretary to check in. "Barry MacNorris, I believe he said his name was."

"I ken he may be keen to see you, too," Tristan said with what struck Lynn as an oddly ominous tone. He really did seem to feel some inexplicable hostility or resentment toward her. He said Barry was away on some estate business at the moment but should be in his office in the old gamekeeper's cottage behind the castle within half an hour.

Lynn went up the winding staircase, and Melody pulled her into their room.

"Look!"

The high-ceilinged room was beautiful, although a bit sparsely furnished for its size. Canopied bed with curtains of pale amber silk, chaise longue upholstered in matching fabric, one small chair, fireplace with marble mantel and a single painting of a dashing hunt scene.

"Isn't the castle wonderful? Isn't the room wonderful? Isn't *Tristan* wonderful?" Melody asked. She clasped her hands together, fingertips touching her elfin chin, like some small child contemplating presents under a Christmas tree.

Lynn murmured agreement, but there was something about Tristan that bothered her, and it wasn't just his unwarranted hostility toward her. But she couldn't quite put her finger on exactly what it was at the moment.

Lynn unpacked and then found her way out to the gamekeeper's cottage. The rocky pathway was overgrown with weeds. Indeed, now that she was able to take her eyes off the fairy-tale castle, she saw that the grounds, though lovely, were quite wild, almost unkempt.

There was a bell beside the door. She had to ring a second time before the door opened.

"I'm looking for the baron or his secretary."

"I'm Barry MacNorris."

He was as tall and as well-built as Tristan, but his hair was brown and he had no mustache. His dark slacks and white shirt practically screamed stuffy, conservative young businessman, the only spot of color a tie in a plaid that matched the kilt Tristan had been wearing. The clan tartan, she decided. She thought he was probably good looking, but his upper face was half hidden by the extremely heavy, dark rims of his glasses, and his mouth was compressed into a straight line of what she suspected was perennial displeasure.

She could not picture Barry MacNorris in a kilt. He looked bookish and boringly correct, the kind of man who never got his checkbook records scrambled, never over-slept, never got hungry for pizza at midnight. In spite of all that, he lacked nothing in potent masculinity. In fact, there was a certain male intensity about him that Lynn reluc-tantly found intriguing—although it was much different from Tristan's brazen style. If Barry even noticed she was female, it didn't register on what was visible of his face. His curt nod acknowledged her presence with all the warmth of a judge looking down at a repeat offender.

"I'm Lynn Marquet—"

"Ah, yes. The lady of the night."

She'd been planning to apologize for interrupting his sleep, but given this arrogant, almost sneering attitude, she changed her mind. Instead she said with cool aloofness, "I thought perhaps the baron would greet us. Everyone is very anxious to meet him."

"The baron hasn't been feeling well the last few days. Arthritis and gout, and a bit of laryngitis as well. Would you come in, please?"

The office was small, crowded and much more messy than Lynn expected. Barry MacNorris appeared the kind of man who'd have every paper and paper clip in its proper niche, but the desk looked as if it had been caught in a paper snowstorm. Barry did not bother with polite preliminaries. He launched right into formal unfriendliness.

"Tristan tells me you have arrived with quite a crowd, to say the least. You should have informed me that you in-tended to gather up all your friends and acquaintances and bring them along. You have operated in an extremely de-vious manner." Bluntly he added, "I also suspect your ref-erences to the Riviera and Martinique on your calendar were grossly exaggerated."

Hostility was apparently a family trait, because Barry MacNorris's attitude multiplied Tristan's unfriendliness by several degrees. He made "friends and acquaintances" sound like "weirdos and misfits." She suspected Tristan had given him more unflattering information about the group than a simple number. And she had to admit that he was quite correct about the Riviera and Martinique.

She had felt twinges of guilt that she hadn't been more up-front about their share-a-castle plans, but then, darn it, he hadn't *asked*. And, given his sour attitude, she wasn't about to make some humble apology and beg forgiveness.

"It's unfortunate that you were unpleasantly surprised by the size of our group, but you didn't inquire how many were coming, so I was unaware that the number mattered. It would seem to me that you should expect, when you advertise ten bedrooms, that there will be sufficient guests to fill them."

He obviously didn't appreciate this form of logic, although it was difficult to make out much of his expression, given the glasses. She could see, however, that his eyes were that same shade of steel-and-glass blue as Tristan's, apparently another family trait.

"The number of bedrooms was included in the advertisement merely to indicate the spaciousness of the castle," he said with superior disdain, "and the number of persons in your party is quite unacceptably large."

They stared at each other, apparently at some sort of impasse.

Finally Lynn said, "Exactly what do you have in mind, Mr. MacNorris? Leaving some of us sitting on the castle doorstep? Or shipping all of us back on the next flight?" When he didn't answer, she added, "We are, I might point out, prepared to make full payment in advance."

She thought that statement impressed him favorably, although the hard line of his mouth didn't soften, and he certainly didn't go so far as to smile. With stiff-shouldered rigidity he moved behind the big desk that had at least a thumbnail-deep layer of papers covering every inch of surface. He pushed aside a cup half filled with old coffee, a congealing film on top, and finally extracted a registration book from under the papers. He shoved it across the desk as if he'd like to throw it at her.

"If you'll just list each person's name, please."

Lynn tried, but she finally had to admit she couldn't remember all the last names, lending credence to his accusation about her gathering up of "acquaintances." "I can get the names for you later."

"Please do."

For no particular reason, she wondered what he was like when he made love. Given his rigidity, she decided, he probably used a board as a mattress. And maybe a stopwatch, to be certain no time was wasted in unnecessary frivolity. There was a certain intriguing air about a man holding himself under tight control, as if a formidable passion lurked somewhere in there. She studied him speculatively, noting he wasn't wearing a wedding ring.

Finally he said coldly, "You're smiling, Miss Marquet. Do you find something amusing about this situation?"

She hadn't realized she was smiling and instantly made sure she did not continue to do so. She wasn't about to tell him what she was thinking, of course, so instead she said, "If you weren't expecting a mixed group of twenty Americans sharing expenses in answer to your ad, just what were you expecting?"

The question seemed to catch him off guard. He touched the knot of his tie, as if it felt a bit tight against his throat. "Well, perhaps a well-to-do family, with mum or mother-in-law, perhaps an accompanying nanny and maid..."

She had the sudden impression that he wasn't all that certain himself about what sort of guests it would be plausible to expect. Lynn looked at the registration book again, realizing that there were no guest names above the list she had started. And this was page one of the book. He apparently recognized what she was thinking.

"Actually, this is our first experience renting the castle and you are our first guests," he admitted. "So perhaps there are a few kinks to work out. The baron was just rattling around here alone, you see, and thought he might try sharing the castle with a few congenial guests."

"There seem to be a few other MacNorrises 'rattling' around the estate," she pointed out.

"Yes, that's true. The baron is very generous about seeing that kinfolk are gainfully employed."

Until then the rain had been pouring straight down, but a sudden gust of wind rattled a sheet of raindrops against the window. Lynn shivered. The cottage was cold.

"I hope the weather improves," she said. "We're looking forward to using the swimming pool."

"It's been an exceptionally bleak spring, but I'm sure the weather is on the verge of improving. Because we're so far north our evenings here are extremely long this time of year and generally quite pleasant." He paused, as if to take a mental step aside to review his statements, and then added a bit vaguely, "Although it may remain too chilly for swimming."

It may be true that June evenings in Scotland were exceptionally long, but given the state of the clouds, rain and wind, Lynn found it difficult to tell whether it was day or night at the moment. Barry turned on a desk light, and they completed the business arrangements. Lynn noted that some of her traveler's checks had ragged edges. They had been in the same purse compartment with Spike. Barry MacNorris fingered the nibbled edges, but he didn't ask for an explanation and she didn't offer one.

When the transaction was finished Lynn peered out the window, a little reluctant to step into the wind and rain.

More or less to make conversation so they wouldn't be standing there in awkward silence until the downpour let up, she said, "The baron doesn't live in the castle?"

"No, he...actually, he lives here in the cottage. That was how he happened to be so close the night you called. He doesn't like the emptiness of the castle, but neither does he like servants around, so I take care of him here."

Barry didn't look like the sort of man to be personally caring for a sick, elderly relative. Lynn was undecided whether to think better of him for doing so or to classify it as just part of some clever scheme cold-bloodedly contrived to help him latch onto the castle and title.

"The baron seemed a charming man on the phone. Although I must admit his thick Scotch accent was very difficult to understand. Does he like the grounds in their natural state?"

"Natural state?" Barry repeated, apparently wondering if her phrase was a euphemism for uncared for, which it was. "Well, yes, I suppose he does to some extent." He paused, eyeing her with a calculating expression, as if considering whether she was entitled to any further information. "Although we do have a gardener who's supposed to keep things trimmed up."

"Another MacNorris?"

"Yes. Michael MacNorris." He paused again, the compression of his mouth hinting at a certain disapproval of this other MacNorris. "I have to keep after Michael or he doesn't tend to business. I'm apt to find that instead of working he's off hunting for secret passageways in the castle or poking around some old ruins or cemetery."

"He sounds very pleasant and likable." And a lot more fun than *you*, Lynn added to herself. If this rain ever let up, she'd keep an eye out for Michael MacNorris.

"Yes. I imagine you and Michael would get along just fine." The hint of superior scorn was back. "You appear to share a certain careless disregard for responsibility."

"I am not irresponsible!"

"Tricking an innocent castle owner into housing a horde of boisterous tenants is exactly the kind of thing Michael would do."

So, he was back to his annoyance with her over the number of guests. Which reminded her of something.

"What about meals?" she asked.

"What about them?" He adjusted the glasses on his nose and eyed her warily.

"The ad did say breakfast and 'sumptuous' dinner were included. I trust this won't be a problem simply because there are a few more of us than you anticipated."

"We'll manage." His mouth twisted into a grim smile. "Although the meals may now be somewhat less sumptuous than *you* anticipated."

He reached for some papers, obviously a gesture to dismiss her, but his hand brushed the coffee cup. It started to tip and spill, and Lynn instinctively grabbed for it. So did he.

Their colliding hands kept the coffee from spilling on the papers, but the touch was startlingly electric, as if at that moment a sudden hot signal that he was male and she was female arced between them. He peered at her through the heavy glasses as if for the first time considering that she might be something other than a shifty-eyed con woman with the ethics of a shark.

"That was almost a very bad accident," Lynn said. "Coffee all over your important papers."

"Yes. Very bad."

By that time they both realized their hands were still tangled together on the cup. Yet neither of them moved, and their hands remained as if they were clandestine lovers prolonging an accidental touch in public. His fingers felt warm against Lynn's, strong, unmistakably masculine. Then she realized the ridiculousness of this; they, whose feelings for each other were hostile enough to start a MacNorris-Marquet feud, were almost holding hands. Apparently the thought occurred to him at the same time, because his hand jerked back at the same instant hers did.

Lynn fought an urge to rub hers. It tingled, as if the touch had short-circuited the circulation. She had a sudden inkling that Barry MacNorris might indeed have something more than ice water in his veins and a stopwatch under his pillow. Perhaps, if they hadn't gotten off to such a bad start . . . .

A little awkwardly she said, "I'll be going now. I think the rain has let up for a minute."

His face, what she could see of it around the glasses, had a most peculiar expression, like that of a man caught in some uncomfortable position and pulled in two directions at once. She thought for a moment that he was going to say something, but, after clearing his throat and tapping the table with his fingertips, he simply snatched up a handful of papers, effectively dismissing her.

The first meal wasn't Spartan, but neither was it sumptuous. The food, veal cooked in an herb sauce, with berries and whipped cream for dessert, was delicious, but there wasn't a great deal of it. Lynn was no connoisseur of fine wine, but the Dunbars and several others who claimed expertise in such matters said the wine served with the meal was excellent. The ruddy-faced cook peered out at the guests, shook her head and scowled. She, too, apparently hadn't been expecting so many.

When the meal was over, Mark had the maid ask the cook if they could have some potato or taco chips to fill up the empty corners. The ensuing verbal explosion from the kitchen indicated that such uncouth snacks would not be forthcoming from *this* kitchen.

By that time, with the change of times and jet lag, everyone was ready to troop up to bed. That was when they discovered that the castle had been only minimally modernized in certain aspects. There were waiting lines at the three bathrooms.

Still, by the time Lynn and Melody were snuggled deep under a down comforter, fire blazing in the fireplace, Lynn was not at all unhappy. She hadn't been deported for smuggling in a rat, the castle was marvelous and she was warm and reasonably well fed. She was also wondering if there was something about Scotland or perhaps Scottish men—or was it just MacNorris men—that made her react differently here. It had been a long time since she'd felt any potent physical reaction to meeting a new man, and yet it had happened twice to her today.

She was undecided whether to be pleased or frightened. She wanted to fall in love and marry again someday, but she didn't want to do it under some foolish, starry-eyed spell the way she had the first time, a mistake that had gotten her married at twenty to a man who couldn't have been any more wrong for her than if a malicious genie had matched them up. By the time she was out of the marriage she was only three years older in years, but she'd felt at least a generation older in unhappy experience.

She was reasonably certain neither Tristan nor Barry was the right man, even though both had made her feel uncharacteristically giddy and very conscious of both their and her own sexuality. But it took more than a sexual blaze to keep a lifetime of homefires burning.

For a few moments she played with the shocking idea of forgetting the value of commitment, forgetting moral standards that sometimes seemed ridiculously confining and old-fashioned, and rushing headlong into some wild week-long affair with one—or both!—of them. There was a certain wickedly rebellious imp in her that sometimes came up with outrageous ideas such as that. Not that she ever acted on the imp's ideas, of course, except in very minor ways, but there was something deliciously tempting about the thought of blithely carrying on parallel wild affairs with two men she'd never see again. And, for all their hostility, she strongly suspected neither Tristan nor Barry would be immune to a seductive flaunting of her charms.

Then she gave herself a hard mental slap across the cheek. Down, girl! Bury that impulse, deep. That is *not* the real you.

She forced her thoughts away from Tristan and Barry and toward the things she wanted to do in Scotland. See Loch Ness, climb the Scott Monument, wander through Edinburgh Castle. Eat scones and oatcakes and haggis. Buy something in a gorgeous tartan plaid, maybe even find a wonderful down comforter like the one she was snuggled under.

She fell asleep optimistically thinking that the rain would surely let up by tomorrow and she could get on with her plans.

The rain did not let up. There was a filling breakfast followed by a castle tour led by Tristan, who apparently did other odd jobs when he wasn't chauffeuring.

He had facts and interesting historical anecdotes to offer. Some of the lower walls of the castle were six feet thick. The upper windows had originally been mere slits for shooting arrows through. A panel of wood had a bullet hole made a century ago, and there was an accompanying tale of family treachery.

There was an enormous banquet room with long tables, a bedroom done in hand-painted Chinese wallpaper, and the Laird's Chamber, where the old barons meted out justice. Something Lynn found especially interesting was that this room also held a hearthstone in which the barony was invested, a barony that was not hereditary but went with castle ownership. She wondered if that fact had any special significance to the various MacNorrises working for the present baron.

The dungeon was of a rare type called a "bottle dungeon," because of its shape, a tiny, solid-walled enclosure with only a narrow opening at the top through which prisoners were lowered and from which there was no escape. Reva, the writer, was taking copious notes, although Lynn had further doubts about what she was writing when she enthusiastically commented that the dungeon was "a marvelous location for a unique lovemaking scene."

There were displays of antique swords, guns, costumes, armor, paintings and furniture. Lynn had never prided herself on being the world's greatest housekeeper, but even she could see everything was in an almost desperate need of dusting.

Melody stayed right by Tristan, hanging on his every word, but Lynn stood back, not wanting to be distracted by his volatile male charisma. She began noticing several oddities about the castle in addition to the layers of dust.

The hallway walls showed lighter oblongs where paintings must have hung at one time but were now missing. Tristan passed by several rooms, and when Lynn surreptitiously opened closed doors, she found the rooms quite empty. In other rooms she noted variations in carpet wear where she strongly suspected pieces had been removed, and she thought back on her own sparsely furnished bedroom. Odd.

Was someone quietly emptying the castle of its treasures when the baron wasn't looking? Barry MacNorris, perhaps?

Chapter Three

Lunch was not served at the castle, so after the tour they all drove into the nearby village to eat at a pub, Lynn still speculating on Barry MacNorris's role in a possible castle plundering. He'd seemed respectful of the baron on the phone that night, but that wouldn't necessarily keep him from helping himself to some ill-gotten gains.

Tristan wouldn't come inside for lunch with them, so Melody took a sandwich out to him. Lynn had thought about doing it herself, but given his hostile attitude toward her, she suspected he might hurl anything she offered right back at her. Yet, in spite of his antagonistic manner, she sensed a definite male awareness of her. She was riding in the castle car today, and several times she had caught him eyeing her in the rear view mirror. His smiles, however, were all for Melody, although he occasionally awarded some other woman with a sizzling flash of male charm.

After lunch they drove around the countryside sightseeing, Tristan leading the way in the small, unimpressive vehicle that bore as much resemblance to a Rolls-Royce as a splinter of glass did to a ten-carat diamond. As far as historical facts went, Tristan made an excellent guide, but he was unhelpfully vague about some aspects of modern Scottish life. Someone asked him to explain the popular British game of cricket, and his reply was an aloof, "I've never been a cricket man meself." He was equally uninterested when asked if he could play the bagpipes for them, saying he'd never found time to learn the bagpipes, and he merely shrugged with disdain when Kristie asked what he thought of some latest bit of juicy gossip about the royal family.

Lynn more than ever felt there was something not quite *right* about Tristan, some element missing in him as a Scottish chauffeur-guide. There was certainly nothing lacking in the potent masculinity he projected, however. Sometimes he seemed to take a certain pride in using the kilt in arrogant emphasis of it. Lynn speculated on the possibility that he was the MacNorris next in line to be baron, and in an effort to build character the old baron was making him take this subservient role as chauffeur.

Lynn was enchanted with the lovely green hills and lakes and castles...and Melody was enchanted with Tristan...but most of the others simply grumbled about the rain. They soon had even more to grumble about. The accountant, overreacting to an oncoming car, swerved too far to the left to avoid it and ran off the road. In the process he managed to get the wheels on one side trapped in a narrow concrete gutter, and no amount of pushing or jacking would free the vehicle. They finally had to ask a passerby to call a wrecker.

They all got back in the cars to wait, but by that time they were already soaking wet. Windows steamed up and so did tempers.

Occupants of two of the cars decided to continue sightseeing on their own, but their later reports indicated their day had also gone unhappily. They'd tried to explore some old ruins and got even more soaked. Mrs. Dunbar had slipped on a muddy trail and done something to an ankle.

She was not diplomatic in pointing out to her husband in front of everyone that she much preferred city-style night life to taking pratfalls while clomping around muddy ruins, and that this whole "miserable Scottish disaster" had been his idea.

On that sour note, they had dinner. There was more food tonight, but it wasn't as elegant.

Afterward, there wasn't much to do. The only television set was in the big room that, for want of a better word, Lynn thought of as the living room of the castle. There was disagreement about what to watch. Two couples departed for the local pub, and another foursome started a lethargic card game. The rain drizzled down.

Finally Grant Dunbar jumped up with an inspired look on his face. "Let's go swimming!"

"You are out of your mind," his wife said flatly. "It's raining. We'll freeze our butts off."

This was not a particularly shocking four-letter word, but everyone was a little surprised at hearing it from the lips of the elegant-looking Mrs. Dunbar. Her husband did not let it deter him.

"No, we won't. It's a heated pool. Once we're in it we won't even notice the cold or the rain. C'mon, let's do it! Don't be a bunch of wimps."

The older man's enthusiasm, and perhaps a feeling of being outdone by someone twice their age, sparked the younger men into action. Lynn's attitude, after a first reaction similar to Mrs. Dunbar's, was, well, why not? It would be better than sitting around snarling at each other. Then she remembered something.

"Suits, everyone!" she called. She waved frantically to get Grant Dunbar's attention. "Suits are required!"

Lynn's suit was technically one piece, although all that held the crisscrossed raspberry strips together were some brass rings on the sides. She shivered as she changed, unable, at the moment, to remember why she'd bought a suit that exposed so much. The fireplaces were the only source of heat for the rooms, and the fire was out. She'd have to remind Barry or Tristan or whoever took care of such things that they needed more coal, because the brass box was almost empty.

She slipped a white terry-cloth coverup around her shoulders and grabbed a towel, realizing for the first time that Melody was not present. Where could she be?

The swimming pool was hidden in a little grove of trees several hundred feet from the castle. The rain actually let up while they scampered out to the pool, but the chilly air brought shivers and goose bumps. For Lynn, the first look at the pool in the dusky evening light almost made up for the discomfort. It was built among natural rocks, so artfully done that it was almost a natural part of the secluded glade. Heavy-headed white flowers dropped gracefully to the water on the far side.

Mark dropped his towel and enthusiastically plunged into the water.

"E-e-e-ow!"

He just as quickly popped back out of the pool, rather like a rejected cork. But much more noisy.

"That is *ice* water! That is colder than—"

The comparison was explicit enough to make Lynn's ears burn. However, they were the only part of her that *was* warm after she tentatively stuck a foot in the water.

Even Grant Dunbar, after a determined, nonwimp splash to the far side, conceded that the pool was not swimmable, at least not with the rain starting again.

The shivering group headed back for the castle, but Lynn took a detour around the pool. She discovered a waist-high structure partially concealed by the drooping bushes. The equipment in it, considering the number of disconnected parts, obviously was not in working condition. The heating system for the pool?

Lynn then headed for the cottage. This was totally unacceptable. First no Rolls-Royce, now no heated pool. Barry MacNorris had to do better than this. And the gardener hadn't been doing his job, either, because the wet grass she had to plow through looked more like an overgrown hayfield than a lawn.

She stomped up to the cottage door and punched the bell. No answer. She rang it twice more before it occurred to her that she might disturb the baron's rest. She didn't want to do that when he wasn't feeling well, of course.

She turned her back to the door, cold, shivering, frustrated and blaming Barry MacNorris for every bit of her discomfort. But he wasn't there, so she had no choice at the moment but to tromp back to the castle.

On sudden impulse she tried the cottage door. Unlocked. Very well, she'd just go inside and wait for Barry.

The cottage wasn't much warmer than the outside, but she spotted a small electric heater and turned it on. She knelt down beside it trying to get warm.

Several minutes later she heard a sound somewhere in the rear of the cottage, perhaps a back door opening. It suddenly occurred to her that her skimpy raspberry strips were hardly a power outfit for a serious confrontation.

She decided she'd just slip out and return in something more suitable—

Too late. From her kneeling position she could already see legs approaching under the desk. Surprisingly, they were bare-kneed legs, with plaid skirt above and heavy stockings below.

She popped up in surprise. "Tristan, what are you doing here?"

He jumped as if she'd bitten him on a bare knee. He had his hand to his mouth, and for a moment she thought he'd been hurt, but then he smoothed the mustache and dropped his hand.

"I wur lookin' for Barry."

"So am I. Things are really not at all acceptable around the castle."

When she had jumped up, the terry-cloth coverup had slipped off her shoulders, and Tristan's eyes were now traveling slowly from the flare of her bare hips to the diamond of taut skin that stretched from her pelvis to just below her breasts. From there his eyes went to the exposed bloom of breasts not quite contained by the narrow raspberry strips, finally shifting to focus dead center on the strips.

She saw her feminine desirability reflected in Tristan's blue eyes as plainly as if they were talking mirrors...and his expression was all smoldering desire, not hostility.

Almost as if his hand were controlled by invisible strings, he reached across the desk and slowly traced the line of her jaw with a fingertip. The fingertip circled the soft curve of her ear and drifted down her throat. It intersected a raspberry strip, and, as if following a line on a road map, unerringly followed the strip across the slope of her breast, down to the low point between the two strips. In spite of the room's chill she felt a drop of hot perspiration gather there between her breasts.

Lynn's mind worked. It said this was outrageous; this was male arrogance at its most insufferable. It fumed and fussed like some overheated steam engine.

Yet it sent no orders to scream, to jump, to slap the hand away. Or if it did, they were lost in the messages of the senses hurtling the other direction—the feel of the hot tip of his finger burning against her skin, the sight of the steel-and-glass glitter of his eyes changing to blue smoke, the sound of his breathing in the raw silence. Or was that her own ragged breathing? No, because her breath was held, caught in her chest by the power of his imperious masculinity.

His hand moved again, upward, around to the back of her neck, a journey across a thousand nerve endings. For a moment she felt the movement of his palm in a rough massage that sent electric surges down her spine, and then his hand clamped down hard, tilting her head back. In slow motion she saw his mouth move toward hers, felt her lips part.

Scream, protest! one indignant part of her shouted. But then his mouth touched hers and the closing of her eyes drew a soundproof veil across that noisy protest within. The only sounds she heard then were the thudding of her own heart, the small male murmurs deep in his throat, the rustle of papers falling unheeded from desk to floor.

His tongue boldly followed the touch of his lips. It invaded her mouth, plundered it, sizzled her senses and sent her sense of balance reeling. She felt the muscular strength of his lips, the dominating power of his hand on her neck, the tease of his mustache. The kiss made no pretense of tender seduction; it simply, almost shockingly, proclaimed his elemental desire to make love to her.

They were touching only above the neck, but Lynn's responses thundered through her body, a riot of desire as her natural inhibitions with a near stranger went up in flames. She strained toward him, would have fallen across the desk, if he hadn't at the last minute caught her with his other hand.

Somehow, some other message got through the hot mist clogging her brain. Her hand was in a puddle of something wet.

She looked down. Another cup of coffee had been left on the desk. She must have knocked it over, and now coffee was soaking through papers and dripping off the edge of the desk. It made her blink and jerk to her senses as if she'd just discovered herself sleepwalking in some incriminating situation.

"Oh, Lord, Barry's going to be furious." She dabbed ineffectually at the wet papers with a corner of her terry-cloth coverup.

For a moment Tristan didn't do anything. He just stared at her as if he, too, had been under some powerful spell. He touched his hair, smoothed his mustache. The scorching kiss certainly had done nothing to dent the superstud image he usually projected with deliberate arrogance, but at the moment he seemed to have forgotten it. Then, with a swirl of kilt, he disappeared into another room.

When he returned he was carrying a towel and some of his air of superior indifference had returned. By that time Lynn had put the coverup back on and belted it securely.

While they blotted wet papers and wiped up the puddle on the floor, Lynn tried to organize her thoughts into some semblance of their usual order. The whole episode was totally out of character for her, although she suspected that was not necessarily true for Tristan. She couldn't recall when she'd ever kissed a hostile near stranger, let alone done it as if she were ready to sink to the floor and make love with him on the spot. And with not a word spoken between them! There was a certain unreality about it all, as if it had happened in some slow-motion dream sequence.

The best thing, she decided, was to simply ignore the last few moments and pretend they had never happened.

She swallowed, cleared her throat and finally managed to say—just as if they were continuing a conversation that hadn't been interrupted by a momentary wildfire of passion— "But I suppose the problems at the castle aren't your concern. Do you know when Barry will be back?"

He considered that and then said, "No." After another moment's consideration, he added, "I think not t'night."

There wasn't much to do then but go back to the castle, and she had to do it in a fresh downpour. She was cold, wet and goose bumpy again by the time she got to the door. She went directly to her bedroom without checking to see what the others were doing.

Melody was in the room, trying, without much success, to get a fire going. With Lynn's help and the burnt offering of almost a box of tissues, they finally managed to encourage a small blaze, but it did little to take the chill off the room. Here, deep within the castle, there was no sound of the pouring rain outside, but Lynn knew it was there. It was beginning to get to her, too. The only guests who didn't seem to mind the weather were Chris and Christy. Lynn wasn't certain if they even knew it was raining, since they seemed to spend most of their time in bed.

"Where were you this evening?" Lynn asked curiously as she and Melody huddled close to the feeble blaze.

"Tristan and I went for a drive." Melody sounded dreamy, faraway. "He makes me feel so . . . different."

"Different from what?"

"Just . . . different."

Lynn swallowed uncomfortably. Melody had never been one to discuss her sexual feelings. In spite of having roomed together for so long, Lynn really knew very little about that part of Melody's life. But Lynn knew all about the kind of "different" feeling Tristan could arouse; it had raced through her all too explicitly only a few moments earlier. One part of her was indignant that it had happened; another part wickedly delighted in recalling each delicious detail.

"Did he do anything?" Lynn asked.

"He kissed me."

Well, well. Busy Tristan. Kissing Melody and then Lynn only a few minutes later. It was what she might have expected of a man such as Tristan, of course. *Quantity* was the name of the game with superstuds.

Still, Melody's information gave Lynn a peculiar and totally unexpected little wrench inside. Deep down, she supposed she'd had a small romantic thought that perhaps some unique, overwhelmingly powerful attraction existed between herself and Tristan. So much for that adolescent little fantasy, she thought, now thoroughly annoyed with herself for having responded like some love-starved tourist to a meaningless flash of sexual expertise.

"What else did you do?"

"Oh, talked and talked. Lynn, I think I'm falling in love with him!"

"Hon, you scarcely know him," Lynn protested. "Be careful—"

"When we talk, he *listens*. And cares. I've never known someone I can talk to the way I can Tristan."

That brought Lynn's thoughts to a skidding halt. A sensitive ability to listen was certainly not any attribute *she* had discovered in Tristan. An unexpected thought occurred to her.

"Is that what you meant when you said he makes you feel different?"

Melody nodded dreamily.

"Just . . . uh . . . *how* did he kiss you?" Lynn asked a little awkwardly.

Melody touched her forehead. "He kissed me right there, as if I were someone very special, someone to be . . . cherished."

Lynn hardly knew what to think. She'd jumped to the conclusion that the way Tristan made Melody feel "different" was sexual, the way he had affected Lynn herself, but that hadn't been it at all. Melody's Tristan, who listened and gave her a chaste kiss on the forehead, must be a great deal different than both the aloof public Tristan or the smoldering Tristan Lynn had encountered in private, or else he was putting on some complicated act for Melody's benefit. The whole situation, especially the fact that she and Melody were apparently attracted to the same man, confused Lynn and made her feel distinctly uneasy.

They sat there in silence by the tiny fire for several minutes. They hadn't any more fuel to make it larger. Finally, not quite certain whether her motives were protective or underhanded, Lynn said, "There's something a little odd about Tristan, in case you haven't noticed."

"Oh? What?"

Lynn had finally figured it out. "The way he talks."

"Lynn, I am surprised at you." Melody, arms hugging herself for warmth, spoke with the indignation of one who was always open-minded and tolerant. "Simply because someone talks a little differently doesn't make him *odd*. The Scotch all talk that way."

"No, they don't," Lynn insisted. "Tristan doesn't sound like the maid or the cook. Sometimes he doesn't sound

Scotch at all. He just throws in some Scotch phrases now and then, and sometimes rolls his *r*s around as if they were loose marbles. And he seems to know so little about current Scottish life.''

''Perhaps he's from a different part of Scotland than the maid and the cook. Back in the States people from Boston don't sound anything like those from Georgia.''

That was true. The explanation didn't totally satisfy Lynn, but she dropped the subject and brought up another that Melody had never really explained. Why hadn't Melody brought Lance Moriarty, the guy she'd been seeing for most of the past year, along on this trip?

''Surely he must have wanted to come,'' Lynn added. Lance was the most devoted suitor she had ever seen.

Melody admitted that Lance had wanted to come, and could easily have gotten away from his architectural firm for a week. ''But I just felt the need to get off by myself for a while and see things from a new perspective. And now, after meeting Tristan . . .'' Her words trailed off as she stared into the embers of the dying fire.

''Don't get carried away and do something rash or impulsive,'' Lynn warned, honestly concerned about this new, moody Melody. She didn't trust Tristan's intentions, in spite of what sounded like an innocent evening the two of them had spent together. Tristan's brazen treatment of Lynn had been anything but innocent.

Then Melody reverted to her usual cheerful self. ''I should be more like you, I suppose,'' she said teasingly. ''Calm, cool and collected. Sensibly weighing all sides of an issue before making a decision.''

Calm, cool, and collected. It was not the way Lynn would have described herself under the powerful spell of Tristan's kiss only a few minutes earlier. Or, for that matter, even now.

It wasn't until Lynn was under the cozy down comforter, Melody already asleep, that another peculiarity about Tristan occurred to her. His hair and mustache were rough gold, but the hair on those muscular legs, which she'd gotten a closeup view of under the desk, was heavy and dark.

Lynn marched directly over to the cottage to see Barry immediately after breakfast the next morning. She had the full list of names to give him, but her growing list of complaints was what she really wanted to deliver. The bedroom had been glacial without a fire when they got out of bed, and everyone else was also complaining about the lack of heat.

The day was the first that gave promise of being nice, however, hinting that Scotland did have some marvelous possibilities. Sunshine warmed the back of her neck. A lovely mist drifted just above the ponds, the swans gliding through it in dreamy serenity. The air smelled of wet grass and trees. It was a morning for taking a walk with a lover, holding hands, enjoying the fresh-washed world together. Lynn sighed and rang the cottage doorbell briskly.

No answer. She waited, rang again. If she didn't know better—and, come to think of it, she wasn't certain she did know better—she'd think Barry MacNorris was avoiding her.

She glanced around, undecided what to do next. Most of the others in the group were driving to Loch Ness this morning. Lynn would like to see the Loch Ness monster if it chose this day to go public, but she also wanted to catch Barry and insist he take care of these mounting deficiencies.

Perhaps even more she wanted time away from what she was beginning to think of as The Group, in ominous capital letters. The two former business partners, now legal adversaries, had almost come to blows at the breakfast table during a ridiculous argument about whether the broiled half of tomato that always came with that meal counterbalanced the cholesterol in the eggs. There had also been a reshuffling of bedroom partners, and Kristie had moved in with the accountant. And something had definitely come unglued between those newlywed lovers, Chris and Christy.

Lynn suddenly realized that she hadn't walked through tall grass to get to the cottage this morning, that it was now a nicely mowed lawn. A moment later a riding-type mower rounded the far side of the castle. The operator of the machine got off, grabbed a smaller piece of hand equipment from a box fastened to the mower and started whacking away at some overgrown bushes.

This must be Michael MacNorris, the irresponsible ne'er-do-well gardener. It probably had been unfair to criticize his work, she decided, considering the foul weather they'd had. He'd started very early on the grass as soon as a nice day came along. She felt kindly toward him simply knowing that Barry felt otherwise.

As she approached, he was still chopping at the bushes, working with admirable energy if not a great deal of discrimination.

"I do believe those are rhododendrons that just haven't bloomed yet," she pointed out.

He whirled, apparently not having heard her approach. He showed the unmistakable MacNorris family traits in his clean-cut good looks, blue eyes and impressive build, but his brown hair fell across his forehead with appealing carelessness. Faded jeans clung to his lean hips and a cutoff T-shirt stopped at midchest and exposed a muscular midsection.

"Do..." He paused, as if collecting himself, then, with a glance in the direction of the mangled bushes, said, "Do yer think soo?"

"Barry won't like it."

"Who keers whoot Barry likes? Him or his baronship, either one," he said with cheerful irreverence.

"You must be Michael MacNorris. Barry told me about you."

"All good things, no doot." He grinned mischievously, obviously knowing what he said was not true.

Lynn laughed, liking him. "Do you know where I can find Barry? I have some complaints to make."

Michael shook his head negatively.

"I guess I'll just have to try to catch him some other time, then." She was reluctant to leave. Michael was pleasant to talk to, a relaxing contrast to dour Barry, sexually charged Tristan and her own group, as well, where the tensions were beginning to feel as if there might be a shootout at the ol' castle corral. But he did need to get on with his work, so she turned to go.

"Top o' the mornin' to ye," he called cheerfully.

She turned back and looked at him again. He groaned.

"I blew it, didn't I? I'll bet that isn't a Scottish saying."

"I'm not sure. It does sound more Irish."

"May I tell you a little secret?" He suddenly sounded neither Scottish nor Irish.

"I suppose so," she answered a bit warily. Her experiences with the other members of the MacNorris clan had not been totally satisfactory, and she was not certain she wanted to share any confidences with Michael, pleasant as he might seem.

"I'm not Scottish. Well, I *am* Scottish on an ancestral level, of course, but basically I'm Mike MacNorris, American. But just because Barry has a little authority here, he insists I go around talking as if I'd been born with a sprig of heather in one hand and a scrap of the family tartan in the other. 'Giving the guests some local color,' he calls it. He thinks they'll be disappointed if they come over and discover the staff isn't Scottish, after all. But I just can't manage to talk like a native. I sound phony to *me*, so I surely must to you."

"Not necessarily. Most of us aren't all that certain what a real Scotsman should sound like." She suddenly thought of Tristan and her odd suspicions. "What about Tristan?"

"Tristan." Mike repeated the name with a certain disdain. "Tristan thinks he's God's gift to the female of the species. He has masculinity honed to a ridiculously fine edge, don't you think? One of those men who women say undress them with his eyes.''

Michael MacNorris was more astute than his casual appearance indicated, Lynn thought, impressed. He had Tristan pegged. Her skimpy attire hadn't required a whole lot of undressing, but Tristan had certainly made an x-ray...or x-rated...scan of her in the swim suit. And reacted as might be expected of such a man.

''How do Tristan and Barry get along?'' she asked.

''Oh, they tolerate each other. Not much else they can do, actually. Barry's thriftiness frustrates Tristan, who lacks that trait the Scots are so famous for. He hates driving that glorified kiddie car rather than the Rolls-Royce. Of course Barry's nose-to-the-grindstone outlook on life is enough to drive anyone crazy, me included.'' He grinned again.

Lynn shook her head and laughed. Such complicated family undercurrents. Then a thought occurred to her. ''The heating system for the pool doesn't seem to be working. Do you suppose Barry, with his thrifty streak, just shut it off?''

''No, Barry wouldn't do that.'' Mike kicked one of the small tires on the mower. Even to Lynn's inexperienced eye the tire looked on its last few millimeters of rubber. ''The heating system needs some repairs. Actually, what it probably needs is a whole new motor.''

''You feel Barry is honest and trustworthy, then?'' she asked, thinking more of the empty rooms and missing paintings than the pool's heating system.

''Oh, yes. Stuffy and dull as a forty-year report on tomato bugs, but honest. Actually, I'm supposed to be handyman as well as gardener, but the pool's system is beyond my abilities. Which annoys Barry no end, of course.'' Mike sounded as if he took a wicked glee in annoying Barry.

Lynn laughed again. ''Are you all cousins, or what?'' she asked curiously. There was such a strong similarity in physical appearance among the MacNorris men, but apparently physical resemblance was as far as it went. Certainly they were quite unlike each other in other ways.

"Who knows?" He shrugged, then smiled an infectious, carefree grin. "Who cares?"

"You're all very close to the same age."

Mike scoffed at that. "Barry was born a stuffy, thrifty old man. Tristan will always be in some oversexed, macho prime of life."

"And you?"

"Barry says I'm twenty-eight going on fourteen."

With his man-sized physique and impish grin, he looked exactly that, and it was an appealing combination. Lynn reluctantly glanced at her watch. "I really had better be going and let you get on with your work. Barry will have both our heads if you don't get enough done to suit him."

"Wait! Do you have anything planned for today?"

"No, not really."

"Would you like to see some old ruins back in those hills over there? They're a long way from a road and never cluttered with tourists. There's such a wonderful, mysterious feel to the place, as if druids might come out and dance at any moment. It's a rather long hike, but we could take a lunch."

The idea was tempting, but Lynn didn't want to get Mike in trouble. She remembered what a low opinion Barry already had of Mike's lackadaisical work habits. "Won't Barry be angry if you just drop work and take off like that?"

"I'll tell him the mower broke down. In truth, I think perhaps it has," he added, looking back at a strip of grass the machine had only half-heartedly chewed through. "He's gone for the day, anyway. C'mon, let's go!"

Mike's blue eyes danced with a tempting let's-skip-school conspiracy, and Lynn found the idea of spending the day with him far more appealing than stuffing herself into a tiny car with The Group.

"I'll have to put on some different shoes for hiking."

"Okay, while you do that I'll get the cook to fix us a lunch."

"You think she'll do it? I don't think she's very fond of the current crop of guests." The cook did tend to boil vegetables to a disinfected limpness, and she hadn't taken kindly to Kristie telling her that less cooking would preserve more flavor and vitamins. "And she isn't supposed to have to fix lunches anyway."

"I'll turn the full force of my irresistible charm on her," Mike said.

And when he grinned, Lynn could well believe that he could charm caviar and champagne out of the crusty cook if he chose.

She turned to go, but he reached out and caught her arm. "You won't tell any of the other guests my secret, will you? Barry would have a fit if they found out. He's about as much fun as a porcupine with ingrown quills, you know."

"Of course I won't tell anyone if you don't want me to."

He leaned over and kissed her on the nose, a delightfully playful kiss that surprised but in no way displeased her in spite of the briefness of their acquaintance.

"What was that for?"

"Oh, gratitude…and the fact that your nose just looked as if it hadn't been kissed in much too long a time."

That was true enough. She only hoped it wasn't as obvious that some other parts of her anatomy also hadn't received much attention lately.

Chapter Four

Melody was in the room picking up a jacket to take along on the Loch Ness trip when Lynn dashed in. Melody's mouth had a dispirited droop, and Lynn asked what was wrong. She said that Tristan wouldn't be driving today. He'd left word with the maid that he had to take Barry somewhere.

"What are you going to do?" Melody asked when she realized Lynn wasn't going along on the trip.

Lynn explained about her jaunt with the wayward gardener.

Melody clapped her hands. "Oh, that's marvelous! Maybe you and your gardener and Tristan and I can sneak off together sometime!"

"We'll see." Somehow Lynn suspected nose-to-the-grindstone Barry was never going to let *that* happen. No fun was going to take place if he could help it.

Lynn changed to comfortable hiking shoes and put sun-screen on her face. By the time she got back outside Mike was stuffing the lunch into a backpack. He was down on one knee, curve of bare back exposed by the cutoff T-shirt. The rippled line of his spine stood out, long muscles on either side of it. Lynn had the most irrational impulse to lean over and plant a kiss there, in the same playful way he'd kissed her nose. She didn't do it, of course, but the thought tucked itself away in a corner of her mind, like some tempting little treasure waiting to be opened.

Mike led the way to a trail through a forested area behind the castle and then motioned for Lynn to take the lead and set the pace. She caught occasional glimpses of the trout ponds. She remarked on the loveliness of the pair of swans floating there.

Mike cast a less-than-enthusiastic glance toward the swans. "They may be pretty, but they're a pair of thieves. They like shiny things best, but they're apt to take anything. One of them even stole a pair of pliers when I was working on the mower one time. I keep threatening to have swan dinner, but they don't seem worried about it."

One of The Group had chosen fishing rather than sightseeing today. He was industriously casting a line repeatedly into the water. Mike paused to watch for a minute, and Lynn thought for a moment that he was going to go back and say something to the fisherman, but then he just turned and walked on.

"Have you been in Scotland long?" Lynn asked. The trail was wide enough here for them to walk side by side.

"Just a few months."

"Tristan was born here, I suppose?"

"Does Tristan appeal to you?" Mike asked unexpectedly.

Just as unexpectedly, because she was not generally a blushing sort of person, Lynn felt a girlish bloom spreading over her cheeks. She must remember that Mike was capable of these insights, because her thoughts had strayed with unsettling frequency to those charged moments with Tristan in the cottage office. Evasively she said, "I was just curious. My roommate finds him very attractive."

Mike frowned slightly. "Tristan sometimes finds those fluttery, blond cheerleader types appealing."

"I didn't know you'd met Melody," Lynn said, surprised. Then she was a little offended at what seemed a rather derogatory description of Melody. Defensively she added, "Melody may be a little fluttery sometimes, but she's basically a very responsible person, and she's *nice*."

"I'm sorry. I didn't mean to sound critical of your friend. It's just that I doubt Tristan..." Mike hesitated, scowl blotting his usually good-natured expression. "I think you should warn your friend that she shouldn't get carried away with her feelings for Tristan. Tristan is not a solid rock of reliability, and he's not above playing one woman off against another. He has a definite problem with commitment. If Tristan had a pet, it would probably be a satyr," he added darkly.

Lynn couldn't help laughing at this melodramatic condemnation of Tristan's character. She momentarily wondered if Mike wasn't just a bit envious of Tristan, but whether or not that was true, she was uneasily aware of the dangers to Melody's vulnerable emotions if he was correct about Tristan.

"You don't think Tristan feels the same way about Melody that she feels about him?"

"I'm sure of it." Mike's tone was as positive as his words. "Tristan is the kind of guy who can say, 'I'll call you,' to a woman and sound so sincere, yet have no intention of ever doing it."

"Perhaps he simply hasn't found the right woman. What makes you think he has a problem with commitment?"

"He says the word has such an *institutional* ring to it, that it hints of imprisonment within a mile-high chain-link fence." Mike's voice deepened to courtroom somberness. "And I now sentence you, Michael MacNorris, to a lifetime commitment in the institution of marriage, never again to know the glorious joys of freedom..."

Lynn stopped short on the trail. "I thought we were talking about Tristan."

"Oh, we are! Using my name in the example was merely a...convenience of speech. I personally have the highest regard for commitment and marriage." He flung a hand to his heart in a noble display of sincerity and integrity, which Lynn somehow did not find very convincing. Perhaps Tristan wasn't the only one with an aversion to commitment.

"Although I suppose it's possible, if he ever stumbled across the right woman, that Tristan will see commitment to the institution in a different light," Mike added with a thoughtful glance at Lynn.

"It's also, fortunately or unfortunately, depending on your point of view, I suppose, not as permanent an institution as Tristan perhaps views it," Lynn pointed out.

Mike's expression went wide-eyed, mildly appalled. "You mean that you think of marriage as something temporary? Rather than 'till death do us part,' you figure it's, 'till we get bored, wear out the wedding presents or find someone new'?"

"I believe in being practical and facing facts. Marriages fail. What do you suppose is behind Tristan's aversion to commitment?"

"Some men are simply born playboys, you know. Maybe it's an overdose of hormones. Or it might have something to do with unhappily married parents who have stuck together through thick and thin and managed to make themselves and everyone around them thoroughly miserable in the process. That might make one dwell on the darker side of commitment, I suppose."

"You're talking about Tristan's parents?"

"We're discussing Tristan, aren't we?"

This gave her a somewhat different perspective on Tristan, although it hardly excused that outrageously bold kiss in the cottage. Perhaps he wasn't so much hostile superstud as protectively cautious, with a vulnerable center under a rough male shell. Then Mike broke into her contemplations about Tristan.

"I do hope we aren't going to spend the entire day talking about Tristan," he said, sounding rather sulky about her interest in the other man. "There must be more interesting subjects around."

"I was merely curious because of my roommate's interest," Lynn assured him.

"Good." Mike produced a wrapped candy from his pocket. "The baron's specialty, peppermints. Want one?"

She hadn't had a hard peppermint candy in years. She sucked it appreciatively, savoring the old-fashioned, tingly taste. Now another peripheral detail of that kiss from Tristan popped up from her subconscious: his mouth had tasted pepperminty. How come everything seemed to remind her of Tristan?

"Speaking of the baron, we're all disappointed that we haven't had a chance to meet him yet," she said. "Is he feeling any better?"

"I don't think so. But I don't have all that much contact with him."

"I've been afraid I might disturb him when I ring the bell at the cottage for Barry."

"He's a very sound sleeper, so I don't think you need worry about that." Mike hesitated a moment and then added, "But I wouldn't count on meeting him if I were you."

"He's that ill?" Lynn asked with real concern. "He sounded so cheerful and likable when I talked with him on the phone. Perhaps we could do something for him, bring him fruit or flowers or—"

"He's not *terribly* sick," Mike said quickly. "It's just that he's…kind of reclusive. I doubt that he wants to see any of the guests." He seemed oddly uncomfortable discussing the baron, and Lynn suddenly wondered if he was holding something back.

"Are you certain the baron is even at the cottage?" she asked. Something odd was going on here. Perhaps Barry had bundled the baron off somewhere and was trying to take over. She still didn't trust Barry in spite of Mike's assurances about the secretary's honesty. Perhaps the entire trio of MacNorris men were involved in some underhanded conspiracy...although she found that difficult to believe of Mike.

"He might have gone to visit friends in Edinburgh," Mike suggested.

"When he's sick?" Lynn asked, instantly identifying the flaw in that thought. Visiting friends hardly seemed something a recluse would do even if he were well.

"Perhaps he's better." Then Mike grinned like a small boy caught with a frog in his pocket. "Look, I didn't want to make a big deal out of it, but the old boy is a real eccentric. We never know what he's going to say or do, so it's just as well he never wants to see anyone."

"He sounded normal enough on the phone."

"Well, he has his good days. But if you met him now, he might have forgotten all about renting the castle and tell you to get out. Look, won't I do?" Mike asked appealingly. "Do you have to have the baron, too?"

He unwrapped another peppermint candy and held it out to her. On impulse she took it with her mouth, her lips touching his outstretched fingers. "You'll do," she assured him.

They crossed a stream by jumping from stone to stone. Lynn didn't realize until she looked back that the scattered blocks were the crumbled remains of an ancient bridge. It gave her a strong, personal sense of the long history of this land, the stones a mystical physical connection between now and some distant past.

"Do you ever wonder what life would have been like if you were a MacNorris living four or five hundred years ago instead of now?" she asked a little dreamily. "Wearing the tartan colors, fighting for the honor of the clan...."

"Actually, it's my understanding that the fighting men stripped off their tartans and fought naked. I guess I'd be the one standing there shivering and saying, 'Hey, c'mon, fellas, what'd'ya say we put this skirmish on hold until the weather warms up?'" He grinned. "And then, given the fact that I'm a rather peaceable type, I'd hope the fuss would blow over before summer and we'd just have a neighborhood barbecue and street dance instead."

"Tell me about yourself in *this* century. Without that old there-isn't-much-to-tell line."

"What makes you think I'd say that?"

"Just a guess."

"Because it's a line you might use yourself?" he suggested with a thoughtful tilt of head. When she refused to admit the accuracy of that, he said, "Very well, then, I'll give you the complete story. I was born on a January 17 some twenty-eight years ago. It was a dark and stormy night—"

"How do you know that?" Lynn scoffed.

"It's always a dark and stormy night on January 17 in Minnesota. And besides, this is *my* story, okay? So, I was born. I grew up. I went to college. I muddled through a couple of unsuccessful careers. I came to Scotland, the home of my ancestors, where I seem to be muddling through another unsuccessful career. Now you."

"I was born in Texas, some twenty-six years ago. It was a hot and humid night. I grew up. I moved to California. I got a job as a secretary." There was a slight omission there, some three years of Larry and marriage and New York, but Lynn did not feel obliged to explain everything on such short acquaintance.

They had walked perhaps two miles by that time, over gradually rising ground, and Lynn turned back to look at the castle towers peeking over the trees. The pool was hidden, but she could see the roofs of the cottage and some old barns or stables.

"Where do you live?" she asked.

"Oh, back that way." He waved a hand in an indefinite direction somewhere beyond the castle.

"Does Tristan live there, too?"

"Yes, Tristan and I share living quarters. Among other things," he added cryptically before saying in a plaintive tone, "*Must* we include Tristan in every conversation?"

Lynn bowed her head in guilty acknowledgement that she had again brought Tristan into the conversation. "Are we still on the castle grounds here?" she inquired to change the subject.

"This was once part of Norbrae, but not in recent times. Much of the land has been sold off over the years. I get the impression that the old MacNorrises were not terribly good at the business end of castle management. Perhaps they were too busy slaying dragons and rescuing maidens in distress."

"Too bad Barry didn't come along earlier. He'd no doubt have whipped everyone into line."

"No doubt." He gave her a sideways glance. She halfway expected him to grumble about her bringing Barry into the conversation, but instead he said, "How do you feel about Barry?"

"I don't think I'd want to be a maiden in distress around Barry. He'd be checking the expiration date on my credit card before he did any rescuing."

"Oh, Barry isn't *that* bad. He's solid, you know, if a bit on the unimaginative side."

The defense, minimal as it was, surprised Lynn. "He seemed to think you and I would probably get along famously. He suggested we both lacked a certain sense of responsibility."

Mike grinned. "I think he's right."

"About getting along or lacking a sense of responsibility?"

"Whatever."

After another couple miles they reached the crumbling ruins of what had obviously been a very large stone structure at one time. It was an open, treeless area, with spectacular views of mountains and a loch in the distance. Parts of the ruins were no more than rocky outlines on the ground, but in other places the old walls stood head high, and a winding staircase of stone steps led to a window in a roofless circular tower.

Mike dropped his backpack and climbed on one of the higher walls. Lynn followed. Flinging their arms out for balance, they edged along the crumbling top edge.

He put an arm around her shoulders to steady her as he surveyed the ruins.

"I say, Minerva, me love, don't you think the castle is looking a wee bit run down these days?"

Lynn jumped gleefully into the act. "Yes, it is m'lord. I keep telling the children they must not be so rowdy in their play, but you know children. And I warned you not to give them that battering ram as a plaything, you know."

"Ah, yes, the children. And how many do we have now, my sweet Minerva?"

"Fourteen at last count, sire."

"Fourteen. My, my." His eyes rounded in theatrical surprise, and then he looked at her sharply. "Hark!" He put a hand to his ear. "Do I hear a band of villains coming?"

He flung the hand to his chest. "Yes, yes, I am hit. Mortally wounded, I fear. Ah, sweet Minerva, just one kiss before I go..."

He dipped his head and kissed her, and his mouth was warmer than the sunshine falling on her upturned face, flavored with the sweetness of peppermint candy. She had no intention of closing her eyes—this was, after all, only a silly game—but they drifted shut. His tongue circled her lips, and they opened under the playful temptation. His tongue found the opening but only flirted with it, teasing her with little darts and retreats.

She played the game with him, returning tease for playful tease, but with her eyes closed her sense of balance on the wall wobbled. She swayed dangerously, but his arm steadied her and then crushed her against him. He started to kiss her again, this time not so playfully, but she pressed her hands against his chest.

"M'lord doth fair make me dizzy," she murmured against his mouth. "That or I've been adding a bit too much Scotch to the broth lately."

"I am failing fast, my love." Mike sank to one knee on the wall, head on her breast. "If I might feel your lips just once more..."

He turned his head up. Lynn gave him her lips, which had a marvelously revitalizing effect. Appreciative sounds rumbled deep in his throat. When she lifted her head he touched her face with his hand, his own eyes still closed.

"Is that you, Minerva, my love? Yes, yes, I'm reviving. I can feel your beautiful face, the swanlike grace of your throat—" His hand dropped a little lower. "The tempestuous curve of your—"

Lynn put a knee to his chest. "Watch it, m'lord, or you'll find yourself splattered all over the estate."

His hand moved back up to more acceptable territory. He sprang to his feet. "Yes, I am most assuredly fully revived. Ah, and isn't it wonderful to hear our fourteen children frolicking nearby?" He tucked her arm through his and gave her a meaningful leer. "What say we toddle off to the castle bedroom and try for fifteen?"

"Not this year, m'lord. I have a splitting medieval headache." She smiled sweetly. "And, unfortunately, aspirin hasn't been discovered yet."

He struck his forehead with an open palm. "Zounds and forsooth and all that stuff." He sighed with melodramatic regret. "I suppose we may as well eat lunch then."

He led the way along the uneven rock wall, but when they were halfway down the ragged end of it Lynn stumbled on the rough surface. Her arms windmilled wildly, and then she plunged forward, shoving Mike off balance when she crashed into him.

Lynn landed on top, sprawled across Mike's back, her fall cushioned by his body on the grassy ground.

"Oh, I'm sorry I was so clumsy! Are you hurt?"

"I'm having a more intimate relationship with a couple of Scottish rocks than I ever really planned to," he muttered. He extracted the offending rocks, and then looked back over his shoulder at her and smiled. "However, the fringe benefits more than make up for any temporary discomfort."

She started to get up, but with an agile twist he turned over to face her. Before she could rise, his hands caught her hips and held her against him.

"You're not hurt at all," she accused.

"Not yet. But I will be if you break my heart." He managed to smile teasingly and look woebegone at the same time.

"Break your heart," she repeated in a scoffing tone. "Are you sure you aren't Irish instead of Scotch? You do sound like a man who's had some kissing contact with that famous old Blarney Stone."

She put her hands on the grassy ground above his shoulders and again started to push herself up, but his arms wrapped around her and held her so she couldn't move. She didn't want to admit it, considering that she thought this a rather audacious action on his part, but his body felt warm and solid and wonderful against hers. She stopped struggling and planted her elbows on his chest. She cupped her chin in her hands and looked down at him.

"This seems a somewhat awkward position for lunch, but I suppose, if it's some old Scottish custom, then I'm game for it."

He kept one arm wrapped solidly around her waist, but with the other he traced the curve of her eyebrow. "Is there some special knight in your life back home?" he asked softly.

"No."

"I can't believe you spend all your evenings pining away alone."

"No. I'm just not involved with anyone. And I don't *pine* even when I am alone."

"But you were deeply involved once?" he persisted. "Involved enough to be married?"

"I took an unhappy spin on the marriage-go-round," she admitted, a bit defensive that he'd so quickly caught her editing an important episode out of her story.

"Want to tell me about it?"

"Not particularly."

"Let me guess, then. You fell in love rather young, married, as the old saying goes, in haste and repented at leisure. You looked on marriage as a monogamous relationship and he considered chasing women as an invigorating form of aerobic exercise. The experience didn't turn you off men completely, but it made you very cautious about them."

How had he guessed all that? It was a remarkably accurate description of the basic differences in attitude that had shattered her marriage with Larry. The hurt of Larry's infidelities was long gone, but the scars were apparently more obvious than she had realized. Or Mike really did have very special powers of insight.

Up close she could see every hair of his thick brown eyebrows, including a few that bristled menacingly at rebellious angles; the slight, not unattractive irregularity of his nose; the strength of his jaw that hinted at a so-far unrevealed stubbornness; the reddish mark above his upper lip where he'd scraped himself shaving; the tiny mole high on his left cheek. They were appealing imperfections, oddly endearing. She reached up and kissed his left eyebrow.

"What was that for?"

"Oh, it just looked as if it hadn't been kissed in much too long a time."

"If you're really interested in kissing all neglected areas—" he began meaningfully, his grin suddenly wicked.

His eyes were the spectacular MacNorris blue, but they had a roguish sparkle the other men's lacked. He smelled of the grass he'd been mowing earlier, with a mingled hint of peppermint, and under it all was an appealing scent of warm, healthy, slightly perspiring male.

She ignored the eager offer about neglected areas and challenged, "Didn't you skip a few pages in your life story?"

"I suppose I might have left out some minor details," he conceded.

"Perhaps you deleted a real-life Minerva or two?"

"Oh, no." He was very firm about that. "Well, there have, of course, been some semi-Minervas, but definitely none of the wedding ring and fourteen-offspring variety. Although I have every hope that my own true love will someday come along. Perhaps she already has," he added with a touch of fingertips to her lips.

"Methinks you're skating on the Blarney Stone again," Lynn said. She once more started to separate herself from the warm cushion of his body, but he showed no inclination to release her. She settled into a comfortable position with her elbows on his chest again, determinedly ignoring the contact lower down.

"Very well, if the items you left out of your life story have nothing to do with affairs of the heart, what did you leave out?" she inquired.

"I can't tell you everything right off," he protested. "Isn't a man more attractive if he retains a little mystery?"

"It's supposed to be a *woman* who is more attractive if she's a little mysterious."

"I'm into equality of the sexes. Equal-opportunity mysteries and all that."

"You're into dodging the subject of what you left out of your life story, and now my curiosity is really aroused," Lynn said.

She felt a movement beneath her as his legs wound around hers and welded her body into even more intimate curves with his. "Is your curiosity all that's aroused?" he challenged with a wickedly sinuous movement of his hips.

Well, to be truthful, no. Mike was an attractive male, fun and playfully sexy. Lying on the cushion of his warm body was not like lying on some inanimate object. A pulse throbbed in his throat, and the hard muscles of his stomach and thighs had a sensuous life and warmth. Her breasts, held away from him by her braced elbows, felt heavy with a desire to press against him. She knew from past experience that she had a normal quota of hormones, though she'd more or less ignored their existence since the breakup of her marriage. And she was suddenly aware that considerably more than Mike's curiosity was aroused.

"What if it weren't just my curiosity that were aroused?" she asked tentatively.

"We might consider... various possibilities for now or later."

She should be grateful, she decided, that Mike was not as boldly aggressive as Tristan, or she would indeed be in danger from an awakened awareness of her body's yearnings. Tristan would act, not consider possibilities.

On second thought, she wondered if her feeling of security wasn't misplaced. Tristan's very boldness was enough to put a woman on guard, but a sweet, playful guy such as Mike might sneak around her barriers before she realized what he was doing.

Determinedly she said, "I'm interested in these mysteries you're concealing."

"Okay, you get three guesses," he said. "What do you think my secrets are?"

"What do I win if I guess correctly?"

He grinned. "Me."

"And if I don't guess correctly?" she inquired.

"Then you get the consolation prize."

"Which is?"

"Me. See? You really can't lose."

"I may decline the prizes," she said primly, "but I'll make a few guesses about your deep, dark secrets. One: You spend your spare time plotting new ways to drive Barry crazy."

"True," he admitted. "A favorite pastime. But there isn't much challenge to it, because it's so easy to do."

"Two: This handsome human-male exterior is really a clever disguise for the eleven tentacles and three eyes you possess as an alien from outer space."

"Preposterous."

She wasn't so sure of that, given the unbreakable clutch he had on her, but she let it pass. "Three: You have some unspeakable, out-of-control addiction to . . . peppermint."

"Absolutely correct. Two out of three, and we have a winner! You may claim your prize, Miss Marquet." He flung his arms wide. "I'm all yours. Take me."

"I think I'll just take lunch, thank you."

But he wasn't paying any attention to her declining of the prize. His arms were back around her, and he was looking at her mouth. "Kiss me, Lynn," he said huskily.

"I will not. The game is over."

"Kiss me."

"No . . ."

But she did kiss him. She could no more have kept from kissing him than she could have stopped a midair fall from a castle window. By fractions of an inch her mouth dropped toward his, pulled by some irresistible mouth-to-mouth gravitational force.

Yet she determinedly kept the kiss light, no more than a fleeting imitation of an intimate caress.

"Lynn . . ." It was reproach and command and plea all wrapped into one husky word. And again her mouth descended to his.

And this time, when her lips touched his, he gave a small, throaty rumble and lifted his head to claim her mouth in a total kiss. With his mouth still on hers, he reversed their positions, capturing her beneath the sprawl of his body, deepening the kiss so that she felt she needed to clutch something for balance even though she was flat on the ground.

His tongue wasn't playing this time. It probed her mouth with the intensity of passion. Her blouse had scooted up, and she felt the heat of his bare torso against her own exposed skin. He slid one hand along her side in a long, gliding caress from flare of hip to just below her breast. Ground that should have felt cold and damp beneath her was instead like a steamy carpet cradling her against him. On the third stroke his hand didn't stop below the breast.

Almost reluctantly she caught his hand before it could do more than encircle her breast with tempting pressure. Firmly she moved his hand back to her waist. "We came here to explore the *ruins*, remember?" she said against his lips.

He reluctantly slid to one side and braced his head on a bent arm. "Oh. Yeah. Right. The ruins. I'm fascinated by ruins." But he wasn't looking at the ruins. He was looking at her, exploring her with his gaze. One fingertip drew circles on the bare skin at her waist, and one blue-jeaned leg still held her legs trapped.

"And lunch," she reminded.

"Right. Lunch. I'm famished."

But he made no move to get up and retrieve the back pack. His hand was still on her bare midriff. She could feel the separate imprint of each fingertip. In fact, she was so acutely aware of his touch that she thought she could feel every whorl of each fingerprint. Tristan might be the expert at smoldering, clothes-dissolving looks and bold, silent kisses, but Mike was no slouch at generating tingles of his own.

The MacNorris men each had their own personal brand of appeal, she realized. It had been a long time since she'd felt any strong stirrings of attraction for a man, the kind of stirring that made her go hot and weak and light-headed. But an accidental touch of Barry's hand had sent electric tingles rushing through her and being solid and reliable was also an asset not to be ignored, as she well knew from past experience. Tristan had set her ablaze with a single kiss, and Mike ... Mike was the most dangerous of all, because, with the clarity of reading a headline, she suddenly knew she could fall in love with him. And where could that possibly lead in the single week they had to share?

She covered the moment of awareness with a tart comment. "You know, if you moved as fast with your gardening as you do in some ... ah ... other situations, Barry couldn't possibly complain about your work."

"Doesn't it occur to you that we have only a week to get to know each other?" he asked, repeating her own silent thought. "That we have no time to waste?"

He finally allowed her to extricate herself from his arms and legs, and she stood with hands on hips looking down at him. He was on his back, hands crossed under his head for a pillow. He should have looked vulnerable in such a position, but he didn't. He looked sexy and lazily calculating, as if he were considering grabbing a leg and pulling her down beside him again.

"If we aren't careful, we'll be nothing more than passing ships in the night. Star-crossed lovers adrift on the sea of life, mourning what might have been." His cheerful smile belied the mournfully melodramatic words. "Are you going to let that happen?"

"I think I'm getting woozy with all this talk of passing ships and seas of life." She put a hand on her stomach.

Mike rolled his eyes. "I'm talking romance of the century, and all she can think about is seasick pills."

Lynn got the backpack, and Mike spread lunch on the ground. She sat cross-legged to eat. He parked himself directly in front of her, knees touching hers.

Lynn picked up a ham-and-cheese sandwich. "So, since you're apparently not going to tell me your deep, dark secrets, tell me about these unsuccessful careers you muddled through. Or are they your secret?"

"Oh, no. My failures are right up front for everyone to see. First I wanted to be an actor. I was in a few college theatrical productions, the leading man, no less, so I thought I was pretty hot stuff. I dropped out of college and took myself off to New York, where reality and my high opinion of my acting talents collided headon. My biggest part was playing Death in a far, far off-Broadway play, where our largest audience consisted of eleven friends. And, since there were twelve in the cast and crew, that meant someone couldn't even coerce a friend into coming."

"How does one play Death?" Lynn inquired.

"Our writer-producer-director envisioned Death as this purple-shrouded figure with two ghostly, white-rimmed eyes peering out. I flitted around the stage looking like an oversized kid out trick-or-treating on Halloween. However, after playing Death in a purple satin sheet, I figured there was no where to go but up."

"And?"

"I was wrong, of course. I hitchhiked out to California, ready to take the movie-and-television industry by storm. I got a few minuscule parts. A nonspeaking chauffeur here, a delivery man there. I was a dead body in a car, a poker player in a television Western. I was—" He groaned. "I was one of a pair of talking toes in an athlete's foot commercial. We wore these bulbous pink outfits and scratched against each other until a shower of healing powder hit us from above."

"And a fine toe you were, I'm sure."

"Not really," he said gloomily. "I lost the part because I kept sneezing whenever they dumped the powder on us. A sneezing toe did not appeal to the client. Wounded his esthetic sensibilities, I suppose. He said my heart wasn't really in the part."

"A heart doesn't fit well into a toe," Lynn agreed. She primly tried to keep her sympathetic smile from turning into a belly laugh.

"So, the talking toes finished career number one. Which was probably a good thing, or I might have spent a lifetime playing various chatty anatomical parts."

Lynn helped herself to a buttery-rich piece of Scottish shortbread. "And career number two?"

"I decided I'd had enough of the hand-to-mouth existence in acting, especially when all too often there was nothing in the hand. I would be very practical and get into something where I could make an honest-to-gosh *living*. So, working part-time at a hamburger joint, I went back to college and studied business administration and computer science."

Lynn nodded approvingly. "Very practical, indeed."

"Right. And, if I may cast modesty aside for a moment, I was the best in my class. I was courted and finally seduced by one of America's leading corporate giants. I had my very own office, my very own computer and my very own staff, each of whom had their very own computers. I had a health-insurance plan and a pension plan and a company stock-investment plan, and no one counted how many trips I made to the water cooler each day."

"The job made you thirsty?"

"The job bored me out of my microchips, and my office was my very own air-conditioned, designer-decorated prison."

"So you quit?"

"Let's just say the company and I came to a parting when they discovered I used my after-hours time to invent computer games."

"Why should they care what you did after working hours?" Lynn asked, feeling a bit indignant at this invasion of privacy. "That doesn't seem fair."

"I was doing it on the company computer," he admitted. "And then a joker friend of mine punched a few keys and put a section of one of my games into a company report, and the corporate blood pressure zoomed sky high. A narrow-minded attitude, don't you think? Time monsters from the Mesozoic era certainly made people pay more attention than they usually did to dull reports."

"Very narrow-minded of the company, I'm sure," Lynn murmured. Mike MacNorris was not the type of man to be wedged into a corporate mold, that was obvious.

"After I made my apologies, redid the report and left the company, I had some interesting discussions with another company that handles computer games. But about that time I had the...ah...opportunity to come to Norbrae, and so here I am. I love the old castle, but..."

"But?"

"Castle life has its...complications." It was a vague answer, one that aroused her curiosity, but at the same time a certain tone said he wasn't going to elaborate on the subject. He lifted the container of tea questioningly and she nodded for more. "So now you tell me about your career."

"It isn't really a career. Although it's an excellent job. I'm secretary to the assistant sales manager of a greeting-card company."

"You don't sound terribly enthusiastic about it."

"It's a good job," she said, a little annoyed with herself that the words came out sounding defensive. She had thought a time or two about leaving SunnyDay and trying something more creative or interesting. But the idea of abandoning solid security for some shaky independence or excitement had always stopped her. She had health insurance at SunnyDay, regular, if tiny, raises, and the company wasn't about to go bankrupt tomorrow and leave her without a job and penniless. The panicky experience of learning, when her marriage to Larry broke up, that he'd taken the comfortable cushion of savings she thought they had and lost it all in some wild stock-market dealings, had been a devastating lesson. She'd come out of the marriage with nothing. The job at SunnyDay had been a lifeline she'd eagerly grabbed on to.

"A good, secure job," she repeated.

"Ah, yes. Security." Mike gave a sage old philosopher's nod. "The world's biggest myth."

For the first time, she found herself mildly irritated with him. "You say *security* as if it were a dirty word."

"No, just a totally inaccurate one, because security doesn't exist. Except perhaps in your faith in yourself."

"That sounds awfully deep coming from a man who once faced the world as a toe with athlete's foot," she teased lightly. Yet she saw a certain truth in it. She'd once thought herself secure in her marriage to Larry, and then found she had only herself to depend on.

"A talking toe gets no respect," he agreed with a regretful sigh.

"Do you have faith in yourself?" she asked curiously.

"Yes, surprisingly enough, considering the circumstances, I do." Wryly he added, "Although the other parts of my split personality sometimes cast dissenting votes."

Lynn laughed and shook her head. Sometimes Mike seemed as open and uncomplicated as a small boy playing hooky. A minute later he could be one-hundred-percent sexy male, eager to seduce her. And a minute after that he might be so expertly evasive that she could even believe he really did have deep, dark secrets.

They stuffed the remains of lunch in the backpack and played a game of knight scaling tower wall to rescue maiden in distress.

Holding hands, they hiked back to the castle in the golden sunshine of afternoon. Mike kept her laughing with more tales of his acting days.

When they reached the castle, the mower was waiting where Mike had abandoned it. He regarded it as if it were an adversary.

"I never realized a machine could look so accusing. I suppose I'd better try to get it running. Are the other guests complaining about how the grounds look?"

"I haven't heard them say anything." But that reminded her that there were several other important complaints she simply must discuss with Barry. "It was a marvelous day, Mike. I had fun."

"Lynn—" He took both her hands and looked into her eyes as if he were about to say something very important. But then he just kissed her lightly on the cheek. "Remember now, I'm a native Scot to everyone else. Mustn't deprive them of their local color."

"Of course."

She waited, expecting him to suggest their getting together again. When he didn't, it occurred to her that perhaps he felt uncomfortable about his status as a gardener-handyman employee and hers as guest.

Tentatively she said, "My roommate thought perhaps she and Tristan and you and I could go to a pub or sightseeing or something."

"No." The rejection was so immediate and sharp that Lynn was rather taken back by it. "What I mean is, I just don't think that would be a good idea at all. It just wouldn't . . . work."

"I see."

"No," he contradicted, quite correctly, "you don't see."

She waited for some further explanation, but none was forthcoming.

"Look, if—if things don't work out for us here, I'll try to get in touch with you back in the States later on," he said. "Okay?"

"I suppose so," she said a little uncertainly. She hadn't expected the old I'll-call-you-sometime line in international form, especially not from Mike. It put her on her guard. She had already suspected there was considerably more to Mike than appeared on the carefree surface. What she hadn't suspected was that some of those under-the-surface traits might be less than desirable.

"Lynn, I really, really like you." His hands tightened on hers. "I want to see more of you, a lot more. But things are more . . . complicated here than they seem."

She considered that a moment. This wasn't the first time he had used that uninformative word *complicated*. "Something to do with Barry or the baron?" she asked.

"More or less. Look, I really do have to get back to work now."

He kissed her again, aiming first for her cheek but at the last minute changing targets and kissing her on the mouth. It was a sweet kiss, very tender. And it also had a flavor of goodbye in it.

Chapter Five

Lynn walked toward the castle, puzzled and disturbed by this odd turn of events. As he had phrased his feelings for her, she "really, really liked" him. Under different circumstances, if they had more time, she suspected her feelings could rapidly leap beyond the liking stage. He was sweet and sexy, playful and fun. Yet he also had that occasional undercurrent of seriousness that told her he was more than the lackadaisical gardener Barry saw in him. He may have had temporary career setbacks, but Mike was no failure.

Yet, in spite of his lighthearted air about his deep, dark secrets, there *was* something a bit mysterious about him. And his statement about getting in touch with her sometime later on was much too vague and stereotyped to be reassuring.

When she glanced back from the castle door he was bent over the mower, absorbed in its internal workings.

The Loch Ness travelers had returned. Melody was standing at the bedroom window, droopy because she hadn't seen Tristan. Lynn grabbed a sweater as soon as she entered the room. The day may have warmed outside, but the warmth hadn't crept inside the old stone walls of the castle. And the brass box was still empty of fireplace fuel.

"How was Loch Ness?" Lynn asked. "Did you see the monster?"

No monster, but Loch Ness was magnificent, Melody reported. She was considerably less impressed with her male sightseeing companions.

"They're so shallow and superficial." She wrinkled her nose in distaste. "Being around them made me even more aware of how special Tristan is."

Lynn, thinking back on Mike's warning about Tristan, didn't know quite what to say to Melody, who was obviously more enamored of the kilted Scotsman than ever. Lynn's own feelings toward Tristan were now wary, although hardly indifferent. The thought also occurred to her that perhaps Mike should have warned her about himself. Her heart wasn't broken, considering how briefly she'd known him, but it definitely felt deflated and hollow after the way the day had ended. She was well aware that the MacNorris men definitely had the potential to be world-class heartbreakers.

"Lance isn't shallow or superficial," Lynn pointed out, trying to get Melody's mind off Tristan and back on her old faithful suitor.

"I know. But..." Melody let her objection to the devoted Lance trail off uncompleted. Then, in an obvious attempt to change the subject, she asked, "How was your day with Mike? What's he like?"

"We had a terrific day. He's nothing like Tristan," she added cautiously, remembering her promise not to reveal Mike's American background. "But you must have met him. He seemed to know who you are."

Melody shook her head. "I don't think so. Perhaps Tristan mentioned me to him." That thought appeared to cheer Melody, but Lynn had a sudden unhappy suspicion.

"Did you say anything to Tristan about me?"

Melody started to shake her head but then stopped. "Yes, maybe I did. Actually, come to think of it, he asked about you."

"And you told him I'd been married, and that my ex-husband was the Don Juan of the yuppie set."

Melody looked stricken. "Yes, I guess I did. Oh, Lynn, I'm sorry! I didn't mean to reveal anything I shouldn't have. It's just that Tristan is so easy to talk to...."

Lynn wasn't angry with Melody. For whatever devious reasons lurked behind that kilted exterior, Tristan had deliberately pried into her private life. And then passed the information on to Mike. That was how Mike had known she had left some important information out of her life story. He had no sensitive powers of insight; he was simply the beneficiary of Tristan's snooping.

She could just hear it now: Tristan, in that detached, superior tone of his, giving Mike a graphic description of her physical assets, telling him that Lynn was a hot American divorcee, simmering with all sorts of repressed urges because she'd been without a man for so long. A deduction she'd no doubt encouraged with her high-voltage reaction to Tristan's kiss. So Mike had jumped right in, expertly plying her with playful charm, ready and eager to exploit any sexual vulnerabilities he might uncover.

And when his attempt at a quick, sizzling romance hadn't worked, he'd decided to dump her. No doubt to concentrate on a more cooperative target. Damn him! Damn them both!

She was ready to run back down the circular stairway and wrap that mower around Mike's neck. If there was one thing she hated it was men who discussed and treated women as if they were revolving trophies to be polished and enjoyed for a night...or a week's vacation.

Suddenly a screech broke into Lynn's anger. She threw the door open. The maid was standing in the hallway several doors down. Her eyes were closed, fists clenched, and she was screaming as if she'd just found a body on the stairs. Lynn raced to her, Melody following.

"What's wrong?" Lynn yelled to make herself heard over the screams. "What's the matter? Are you hurt?"

Then Melody pointed out what was wrong. Spike the rat was peeking out from the woman's curly red hair, looking as if he, too, would scream if he could. Lynn disentangled the rat, but the woman kept combing her fingers through her hair as if she thought other creatures might be lurking there. She babbled some half-hysterical story about bringing an extra blanket up to the room and having the rat leap off the bed at her.

Spike, apparently now feeling more secure, snuggled against Lynn's body. She could feel his little heart racing madly.

"It's okay. He's just a little pet," Lynn soothed. "He was probably just lonely."

She held Spike up to show how harmless he was, but the maid was having nothing to do with rats. She threw up her hands and fled, muttering something about crazy Americans.

By that time various other people, having heard the commotion, had arrived. Lynn was rather surprised at who came out of the various rooms. Apparently some further reshuffling of bedroom partners had taken place.

Lynn returned Spike to his cage. The wire door was open, but whether that was an accident or Mark just letting his rat roam free, she didn't know.

Lynn and Melody went back to their room, but it was too cold to stay there. They went down to the main living room, where there was still enough coal to keep the fire going. Lynn warned Mark that he *must* monitor his rat's activities more carefully. Then, in what was becoming an all too familiar trek, she went over to the cottage. Again Barry didn't answer the ring of the bell. Mike had gotten the mower going and was churning through more tall grass, no doubt taking down any flowers or shrubs that were unfortunate enough to stand in his path. She had no desire to talk to him at the moment, but he waved to get her attention. He cut the engine when he was a few feet away.

"Lynn, I've been thinking, and—"

She cut him off briskly. "We're freezing to death in our rooms because there's nothing to burn in the fireplaces. I can never locate Barry, so would you please tell him to have some coal or wood delivered to the rooms immediately, or do it yourself."

"Well . . . uh . . . actually, I'm not sure there is anything. I think Barry expected warmer weather by now."

"Then we need electric heaters like the one he has in his office."

"Lynn, is something wrong?" Mike asked.

She didn't give him unearned credit for sensitivity or intuition for pulling that brilliant deduction out of her icy attitude, and she deliberately misinterpreted his question. "I've just told you. The rooms are so cold that it's like living in a castle-shaped iceberg."

"Besides that. Something wrong between you and me."

"Why don't you discuss it with Tristan?" Lynn retorted.

She turned and started to stalk back to the castle, but he jumped off the mower and came after her. He grabbed her arm when he caught up with her and swung her roughly around to face him.

"What's that supposed to mean?"

"I'm sure you're clever enough to figure it out. It also occurs to me that never in the course of this day did I actually tell you my name. Yet you knew it, of course. Along with all those other details of my personal life that were none of your business."

"It's part of my job to know guests' names."

That explanation didn't carry much weight with Lynn, but she gave him a chance. "And who is that?" she asked, motioning toward Grant Dunbar, who was walking across the cut grass toward the secluded swimming pool.

"Okay, so I can't remember them all," Mike muttered. His hands slid up to her shoulders, thumbs lightly caressing her throat. She disregarded the treacherous reaction of her skin and held herself stiff and unresponsive.

Mike's fingertips moved around to massage the back of her neck. "Lynn, look, there is a reasonable explanation for everything, but it's kind of complicated—"

She was distinctly tired of hearing that word *complicated*, which explained exactly nothing.

"I don't think there is anything particularly complicated about you and Tristan discussing female guests with an eye for who's ripe for plucking. Do the two of you draw straws to see who gets whom? Or do you just settle for Tristan's discards?"

Dinner had all the stretched-tight atmosphere of a rapidly collapsing international conference. The Dunbars weren't speaking to each other, but Chris and Christy's noisy argument about each other's sloppy living habits more than made up for the other couple's silence. Reva announced darkly that some of the notes on her new novel were missing, with the obvious implication that someone had stolen her literary masterpiece. The maid, who also served as waitress, was noticeably absent. Lynn and Melody filled in as waitresses for the meal.

The man who had spent all day fishing complained sourly that there were no more fish in the trout ponds than there were in the castle bathtubs. He was also unhappy with the swans. One of them had stolen a pocketknife out of his fishing box and, after deciding it was inedible, blithely dropped it in the middle of the pond. His live-in mate then announced with equal acidity that if she'd known all he intended to do in Scotland was fish, she'd have come alone. He responded that in the early part of their relationship she'd pretended to *love* fishing. Their vitriolic glares at each other could have dissolved lead weights.

Yet in spite of the sparks and tension, no one left the room because it was the only place in the castle that was even semiwarm.

Into this uneasy atmosphere Reva suddenly announced brightly, "I have a terrific idea. Let's play a game!"

Groans. Derisive remarks. Loud comments about *hating* charades. Even the Dunbars united long enough to agree that parlor games were the epitome of social no-man's-land.

Reva didn't back down. "No, no, you haven't even heard yet. It isn't charades. This is a terrific game. It's called Murder."

She explained the basics of the game. Each person selected another person whom he or she would most like to murder. They would then scatter to various parts of the castle and track each other down, no one knowing who was after whom, although people could join forces if they wished. Afterward, the "dead" losers would treat the winning survivors to midnight snacks at the pub.

Lynn thought the whole idea sounded morbidly dumb and utterly ridiculous, and she wanted no part of it. She assumed the others would feel the same way, but after some initial grumbling, the idea seemed to catch on. Murder apparently held a definite appeal. People were giving each other covert glances and sometimes even openly calculating looks.

Reva elaborated on the rules of the game, and there was some discussion about how successful murderers would mark their victims. The decision was to use ballpoint pens to draw an X on the murdered victim's forehead. A bunch of people chasing each other around in the dark with ballpoint pens poised for attack struck Lynn as even more ridiculous. When Reva passed around a cup into which each person was supposed to place a slip of paper naming an intended victim, Lynn donated a blank piece.

She considered just disappearing upstairs and going to bed, but she wasn't wild about the idea of someone sneaking in and pouncing on her with a lethal ballpoint pen. Instead she slipped out the back way, leaving the others to their game . . . and hoping no one got carried away and turned game into reality. She already suspected that Reva had invented the game on the spur of the moment to stir things up and further her "research."

Outside the castle the evening was decidedly cool, but at least it wasn't raining again. The time was after ten o'clock, but the dusky light of a far-northern-spring evening lingered, the kind of light that made Lynn feel as if ghosts flitted just beyond her perception. She strolled out to the swimming pool, stuck a hand in the water and found that it still felt as if it had been there since the last ice age. She shivered, wishing she'd brought a heavy jacket, but she didn't want to venture back into the castle to get it.

She walked to the trout ponds, motionless as dark mirrors, idly wondering where the swans went at night. Lights gleamed softly, romantic and mysterious, in the fairy-tale silhouette of the castle. She wished Mike were there to walk with and talk to. . . .

No, she didn't, she chided herself firmly. Mike was not the man she had originally thought he was.

When she saw cars leaving the castle, which she hoped signified no serious casualties from the game, she headed back in that direction. The moon had risen by then, hazy and romantic in a gathering mist. She heard a noise as she passed the gamekeeper's cottage. At first she thought it was some unfamiliar night bird, but then she realized it was a cat. The cry was plaintive, obviously a plea for help. She followed the sound until she could see its source.

The cat was on the roof of one of the old stable buildings near the cottage, a moving silhouette as it ran back and forth trying to find a way down. There were trees close to the rear of the building. The cat must have climbed a tree, jumped to the roof, and then found it couldn't return the same way.

Lynn moved a little closer. She couldn't see any way she could help the animal, but she was reluctant simply to abandon it. It might try to jump from the high roof and injure itself.

She glanced at the cottage. The windows were dark. Barry and the baron must already be in bed, although the cat's yowls sounded loud enough to waken the soundest sleeper. Perhaps Barry had never returned from wherever he'd gone earlier.

She spotted a line of garbage cans beside the cottage. Perhaps if she stood on one of them she could reach the stable roof and rescue the cat.

She dragged an empty garbage can over to the stable, but when she turned it upside down and climbed on it she still couldn't reach the roof. She wrestled another can over and piled it on top of the first one, but the two cans were then too unstable to stand on. One more can, and she finally had a climbable pyramid of three cans.

She scrambled to the top, grabbing the edge of the roof to steady herself. "Here, kitty, kitty," she called softly.

The cat came running. She scooped him into protective custody, reassured him with a few strokes on his soft fur, and then started to edge down from her precarious position. She was on the bottom row of cans when the cat suddenly realized he could make it to safety by himself from there. With a cavalier lack of gratitude for her rescue effort, he squirted out of her arms and leaped for the ground. His abrupt jump shoved Lynn off balance. Her arms gyrated wildly as she tried to keep from falling.

She and three metal garbage cans tumbled to the ground in a crash that sounded like a class of second graders set loose in a roomful of drums and cymbals. One can crashed merrily into the stone cottage. Another bounced off the stable wall. The third made an elaborate loop before careening with what seemed like gleeful accuracy into the remaining cans standing by the cottage. The sounds reverberated through the night, echoing like the start of some medieval attack on the castle.

Lights instantly flashed on in the cottage and a curtain flew open. Lynn, sprawled on the ground, head whirling dizzily from her fall, thought two figures dashed around the corner of the building. She blinked and shook her head to clear it, and the two figures merged into one.

One male MacNorris figure, bottom pajama clad, chest and feet bare, hair disheveled. Expression incredulous.

His glasses were askew on his nose, apparently plopped there in haste, and he straightened them. He ran his fingers through his hair, bringing it back to a semblance of its usual neatness. Light streaming from the cottage windows gleamed on his bare skin and dark chest hair.

Oh, Lord, she'd done it again, she realized. Wakened Barry in the middle of the night. He was looking at her as if undecided whether to check and see if she was injured . . . or stuff her headfirst into one of the garbage cans.

Under the circumstances, she decided that attack was the best form of defense. "I've been trying to get hold of you since yesterday, but you're never around. Several matters concerning our rental of the castle are quite unsatisfactory and really must be attended to."

An attack made from an undignified, sprawled-on-the-ground position lacks a certain assertiveness, however, and Barry did not appear impressed.

He folded his arms across his bare chest and stared down at her. "Well. The lady of the night strikes again. May I ask what you were doing out here? Perhaps looking for something incriminating in the garbage cans? Or merely using this rather bizarre method of getting my attention?"

Lynn got to her feet. At the last minute Barry held out his hand to help her. She ignored it and got up by herself. She dusted off the seat of her pants. Her hand came away muddy.

"I happened to be out strolling around and heard a cat meowing for help. I found that it was stranded up there—" she motioned toward the stable roof "—and I was merely trying to rescue it."

"Very admirable, I'm sure. But C.C. climbs all over these buildings, and he's quite capable of getting down by himself as soon as he decides no one is going to respond to his melodramatic cries for help. If I came running every time C.C. yowled, I'd be doing nothing else."

"Oh." So Lynn's noble attempt at animal rescue hadn't been needed after all. The information made her feel even more awkward about the noisy uproar she'd created. In a weak attempt to divert attention from herself she said, "The cat's name is C.C.?"

"Short for Castle Cat." The name seemed a bit whimsical, given Barry's humorless nature. As if to confirm that he'd had nothing to do with it, he added, "Mike named him."

"About these matters I must discuss with you—"

"I suppose we may as well step inside. You're shivering."

Lynn was indeed shivering in the chilly night air, although she was rather surprised that Barry showed even a reluctant concern over her physical comfort. The cold didn't seem to affect him in spite of his bare chest and feet.

Once inside, he saw her looking longingly at the electric heater. After a moment's hesitation, he turned it on.

"Thank you."

No "you're welcome" from Barry, of course. He was probably calculating the cost of electricity per minute. In affirmation of her suspicion he said disapprovingly, "Electricity is very expensive here."

She stood next to the heater. He went around behind the cluttered desk and shuffled some surface papers. On one corner of the desk was the inevitable half cup of cold, scummed-over coffee. Barry looked no less intimidating simply because he was wearing nothing but pajama bottoms. His muscled torso and lean hips indicated that he didn't spend all his time shuffling papers. Then she looked closer, not quite believing her eyes.

There was no mistaking the tiny, dark figures on the lighter blue fabric of the pajama bottoms. "Teddy bears?" she said incredulously. *"Teddy bears?"*

Apparently he also decided that attack was the best form of defense and chose not to discuss his unlikely choice of pajama print. "Your group are definitely not the sort of guests we had in mind when we advertised the castle. From what the maid says, you almost need a traffic cop in the hallway to direct the changing-bedrooms traffic. I might add that this is only one of the comments she made just before quitting her job earlier this evening."

His disapproving look told her he assumed she was involved in the bedroom traffic. Considering that it was none of his business, she chose not to enlighten him. Nor to tell him that she was also rather appalled by the activity.

"The lack of a maid is one of the matters I wished to discuss with you. My roommate and I had to wait on the dinner tables this evening. I believe we have a right to expect—"

"The reason the maid quit, as I suspect you are well aware, is that she encountered a white rat running loose in one of the bedrooms. She was understandably quite upset when it leaped on her, clawed its way up her arm and tunneled into her hair. Since we are not in the habit of keeping white rats in the castle, I can only assume the creature belongs to one of your adolescent-minded friends."

"It's a perfectly harmless pet," Lynn said. Barry's lurid description of the rat's activities made the small, harmless animal sound like some maid-eating monster. Defensively she added, "His name is Spike."

"I do not recall agreeing to allow pets in the castle, no matter what their names may be. The fact that a pet was being brought along was another of the facts you conveniently concealed when you made the rental arrangements."

"Actually, I didn't know about Spike at the time—" Lynn broke off when she realized this information was irrelevant to Barry. His look said that even if she hadn't known, she should have.

"I assume you now have the creature under control?" he added, still taking the attitude that Spike was a major menace to society.

"Yes, I think so." This discussion of complaints was definitely not going as she had planned. Reluctantly she added, "I'm sorry he frightened the maid. I'm sure it was unintentional."

"Also, I would appreciate it if you would inform your friends that bits of the castle are not to be taken as souvenirs. The cook tells me she found one of the women chiseling away at a loose chunk of stone."

Somehow Lynn wasn't surprised. If she ever did this again, she thought grimly, no one was coming along without written character references from employer, landlord, psychiatrist and minister, priest or rabbi. Although, on second thought, she was simply *never* going to get involved in anything like this again.

She swallowed, furious with The Group for such behavior and for putting her in the position of having to apologize still further for their actions. But apologize she must, of course.

"I'm very sorry about that," she said stiffly. "I'll find out who it was and speak to her."

"At the same time, you might inform your friends that sticking chewing gum on the underside of a plate is also not acceptable in polite society. The cook brought that to my attention."

Lynn groaned inwardly. "I'm sorry about that, too, but I'm really not responsible for everyone's personal behavior—"

"*You* rented the castle," he shot back with venomous logic. "Now if you don't mind, it *is* late—"

"Yes, of course. I'm sorry I wakened you—" Lynn was meekly turning to leave before she realized what was happening here. She, who had been trying for some time to locate him so she could voice her complaints, was being summarily dismissed without even being heard.

"Hey, wait a minute! You haven't even given me a chance to tell you what *our* complaints are."

He was looking at a piece of paper on top of one of the heaps covering the desk. Reading upside down, it looked to Lynn like a bill with a past-due notation.

He gave her no encouragement to continue. His unfriendly eyes behind the heavy-rimmed glasses told her that he was not interested in some midnight recitation of frivolous complaints, but she refused to be put off any longer.

"Now, what *I* wanted to talk to *you* about," she began determinedly. "First, the advertisement specifically said a chauffeured Rolls-Royce was included. There is no Rolls-Royce. Second, the swimming pool was supposed to be heated. It is not. In fact, I wouldn't be surprised to see icebergs forming in the corners. Third, the bedrooms are frigid—"

"I doubt that," he said, his meaning clear from the sneer in his voice. He looked down at her as if he were viewing her from some great, morally superior height.

"Regardless of what may or may not be taking place in the bedrooms, the temperature in the rooms is far too cold for comfort because of a lack of fuel for the fireplaces. Considering the exorbitant rate we're paying, icy rooms are also quite unacceptable."

"I see."

"Furthermore, it is obvious that paintings and furnishings have been removed from the castle—"

He didn't bother to deny the accusation. Still firmly ensconced on his mountaintop of superiority he merely stated, "I don't believe that is any of your concern."

"Our room is rather meagerly furnished, to say the least—"

"I really doubt that the antique canopied beds in each of the rooms could be considered 'meager,' especially considering their value."

His look said his patience was being strained by such petty matters. She started to bring up another complaint, that the number of bathrooms was quite insufficient for the number of guests using them, but then she realized that would only give him ammunition for more retaliatory complaints about her having brought too many people to the castle. She went back to an earlier problem he had ignored.

"And there is, of course, the problem of a lack of maid and waitress. In fact, the castle was considerably understaffed even before the maid disappeared."

Again that frustrating, completely noncommittal, "I see."

"So, now that you do see, what do you intend to do about these matters?"

He shuffled papers and readjusted his glasses. If Lynn didn't suspect he had no nerves, she'd think he was nervous.

"Actually, there isn't a great deal that can be done. The Rolls-Royce is...unavailable. The heating system for the pool needs some unexpected repairs and there is a problem obtaining replacement parts. It may take a few days for delivery of fuel for the fireplaces, and also a few days to find a replacement maid." Expertly shifting accusation to her again, he added, "Finding a new maid may be particularly difficult, because I imagine the former one will not be reticent in spreading the word about the crazy Americans staying here."

Lynn refused to retreat. "Be that as it may, it is up to you to find someone. My roommate and I cannot be expected to wait tables indefinitely."

"As for the matter of the missing antiques in the rooms—" he shrugged shoulders that looked broader than ever in their naked state, their intimidating strength not compromised by the teddy-bear pajamas "—some of the excess furnishings and paintings have been disposed of. But I doubt that anyone other than you has even noticed anything is missing." His tone implied that she was being as picky as some fussy matron discovering a few drops missing from the bottle of cooking sherry.

"You're telling me that you're not going to do anything, then?" she asked. "The swimming pool will not be heated, the Rolls-Royce will not be available, the rooms will remain icy—"

"I may be able to get Mike to cut up a tree that blew over earlier this spring."

He spoke as if doing this would be an enormous favor for which she should drop to her knees and thank him, and she was suddenly furious. "I'm sorry, but merely supplying a few sticks of wood will not be sufficient remedy for all the deficiencies we have encountered. Not sufficient at all! And I just remembered something else. The so-called 'trout ponds' are as devoid of fish as the swimming pool is of heat. *Nothing* is as it was advertised."

His throat moved in a noticeable swallow. His fingertips tapped the desk like galloping horses. "I might be able to persuade the baron to make some adjustment in the rental rate, considering these . . . ah . . . circumstances," he finally said.

On sudden impulse Lynn made a new demand. "I would like to talk to the baron personally, if you don't mind."

Barry obviously did mind. With a certain malicious satisfaction, Lynn noted that he looked quite alarmed. His fingers shuffled papers at a faster pace. The coffee cup tipped precariously close to the corner of the desk, but Lynn restrained herself from rescuing it.

"Uh . . . well, as I told you, the baron hasn't been feeling well, and he really can't talk, considering his laryngitis—"

"It won't be necessary for him to say anything. He can nod his head in answer to my complaints, I'm sure."

"I don't think it's advisable—"

"I'm afraid I must insist." Lynn was certain she'd hit on a vulnerable point here, and she was determined to take advantage of it. Barry obviously did not want her to see the baron, but she suspected the reason was something more devious than the baron's physical condition. He had sounded hearty enough on the phone not so long ago. Barry was hiding something, either from her or the baron. Or both. With sudden inspiration she added, "Perhaps I could just pop in on him for a moment right now—"

She had no intention of actually rousing the baron out of his sleep, of course, whether or not he was ill, but she started around the desk as if she fully intended to search the cottage until she found him.

Barry instantly blockaded the way, his body a solid wall of muscle, his arms at stiff right angles to prevent her from dodging around him. She put her hands up when she realized she was going to collide with him, and they landed on his bare chest. She should have jerked them away instantly, but they stayed there as if his chest were exerting some powerful magnetic force. The muscles were hard against her palms, but the silky chest hair curled softly, intimately, around her fingers.

She looked up, expecting to see menace or hostility in his eyes, but something else flickered there. Something she couldn't quite identify, and it confused her because it seemed to hold some unspoken appeal or request for understanding.

And while she was trying to figure that out, his arms moved inward, enclosing her rather than pushing her away. They wrapped around her, unexpectedly molding her to him.

"Lynn, I—I mean—I want—" He shook his head a little helplessly, as if the words were tangled in some alphabetic road block and wouldn't come out. And then he gave up on whatever he was trying to say and kissed her instead.

The kiss was hot and deep. If she had been thinking clearly, she probably would have thought that it wasn't at all the kind of kiss she'd expect from stiff, reserved Barry, that perhaps her earlier speculations about a hidden passionate nature were accurate. But she wasn't thinking all that clearly. She was too astonished by the nature of the kiss, the feel of lips and probing tongue, the faint scent of some pine-scented soap on his skin, the feeling that her heart was throbbing in the very tips of her breasts. Her hands crept up his chest to encircle his neck, fingers against the solid knob of bone at the back of his neck, thumbs caressing the softness of his earlobes.

The MacNorris magic, she thought in some dim, dizzy recess of her mind. She seemed helpless to resist no matter where it came from, no matter how angry or suspicious she was.

He lifted his mouth and looked down at her, but when she tried to speak he cut her off with another kiss. She could feel his male arousal through the thin fabric of the pajamas. One part of her was shocked and a bit indignant, but the part that was in control of her muscles simply pressed closer to him. That part of her didn't want to question or examine this; it only wanted more of this kiss that made her feel as if she were simultaneously drifting and sizzling.

Finally he lifted his mouth again. "Lynn, I don't want us to be arguing and fighting. Stay with me tonight and—"

He had a mole, she realized suddenly. A tiny mole high on his left cheek, visible only in intimate closeup. A mole exactly like Mike's. The unexpected discovery of this similarity hit her like a cold slap between the eyes, jarring her into a shocked realization of exactly what was happening here.

It wasn't only in physical characteristics that the MacNorris men were much alike after all; they had certain character similarities, as well. Neither Mike nor Barry was above using a virile sexual expertise to get what he wanted. Except that Barry's motives were even more despicable than Mike's. Mike had planned seduction for the understandable if not necessarily admirable goal of enjoying a spicy week-long affair with her; Barry was cold-bloodedly attempting seduction to divert her from pursuing complaints that might disrupt his comfortable setup with the baron.

Without saying anything, her hands slid down his body. She deliberately made the touch enticingly distracting, with

sensuous whispers of promise from her fingertips. They
glided through the mat of chest hair, leisurely circled a male
nipple, tantalized the dark line of hair curling to his navel.
He apparently took this as an encouraging sign. His hands
moved up to her shoulders and kneaded them lightly.

Her left hand slid provocatively toward the elastic top of
his pajamas, her right unobtrusively drifted toward the
coffee cup on the desk.

"Lynn—"

She gave him a devastating smile that said her complaints were forgotten, that she was a willing participant in
whatever he wanted. She held his blue eyes with her own, let
her eyelids go half closed with sensuous invitation.

For a moment, as his mouth dipped toward hers again,
she almost abandoned her devilish plan. The desire in his
eyes was tempting, the feel of his hands inviting, the arousal
of his body hotly seductive.

But she knew the ulterior motives behind this clever display of male virility. She coordinated her next movements
with smooth precision.

Chapter Six

Barry's yelp was enough to send any inquisitive medieval ghosts back to their hiding places. He leaped backward and stared at the brown stain creeping across the front of his pajamas.

"You dumped cold coffee on me." He said it with a certain disbelief in spite of the evidence trickling down his leg. Then the words became a roar. *"You poured cold coffee down my pajamas!"*

Lynn fished a clean tissue out of her pocket and made as if to pat the brown stain helpfully. He took another step backward, hands protectively crossed in front of him. His wary look said she might have some dangerous weapon concealed in the tissue. There was now no sign of male arousal within the pajamas. Apparently a drench of cold coffee was an effective anaphrodisiac.

"The whole bunch of you really are as crazy as the maid said," he declared. He shook his head as if he still couldn't believe what she had done.

Lynn also couldn't quite believe she'd done it. It really was rather awful. Yet sometimes those incredible impulses did come over her, as if some internal imp grabbed control. She resolutely did not apologize, however.

"I didn't feel you were taking my complaints seriously. Perhaps now you will. I want to talk to the baron."

"That really isn't possible—"

"He's surely awake, after all the noise you made. *If* he's even here."

Barry glowered at her, hands still crossed in front of him as if he didn't trust her intentions toward that most vulnerable portion of male anatomy.

Finally, with obvious reluctance and a dark scowl, he said, "Very well, but not tonight. If the baron is agreeable and feels up to it, I'll suggest he come over to the castle and have dinner with all of you tomorrow evening."

The abrupt surrender surprised her. "Well, uh, that will be fine. Great! I'll tell the others, and we'll look forward to meeting him."

"Good. Now if you'll just *go*—"

Brown liquid had reached his ankles. Lynn started to say something, decided she'd better quit while she was ahead, and fled.

By morning, the rain was back. Lynn and Melody again had to fill in as waitresses, both of them aware how efficient the real waitress had been because it took two of them to take her place.

The game of Murder had not improved relations within the group. There were dark looks, murmurs about cheating, tense references to inadequate rules. Someone asked suspiciously what had become of Lynn during the game, and she murmured an evasive answer about getting turned around in a dark hallway. She brought up the subject of someone trying to remove bits of stone from the castle as souvenirs, but no one would admit to having done it.

Her announcement that the baron was coming to dinner that evening did brighten the atmosphere a little, if only by providing a fresh topic for discussion and speculation. She only hoped he would actually show up, that Barry wouldn't somehow squirm out of providing the baron's presence as he had squirmed out of providing the Rolls-Royce and heated swimming pool. She did not think the shaky status of The Group could stand another evening of Murder; next time there might be real bodies scattered around.

After breakfast, several people decided to drive to Blair Castle for a tour. The decision was made, Lynn suspected, not so much on the basis of the huge variety of antiques a guide book said was on display there as on the fact that it would be a *dry* tour, not a wet scramble through crumbling ruins. Melody, because Tristan seemed to have dropped from sight, reluctantly decided to accompany Kristie on a search through Edinburgh's shops for antique keys. Lily Dunbar settled on a centrally-located sofa with a book, pointedly coughing and clutching a box of tissues and bottle of aspirin to let her husband know that this trip, *his* trip, had put her on her deathbed.

Lynn bundled up in a jacket and rainscarf and headed out alone to explore the old stone outbuildings beyond the gamekeeper's cottage. The rainswept air was so fresh and invigorating that she really didn't mind the falling raindrops. All the outbuildings were locked up, however, so it was not a particularly fruitful exploration, although she did enjoy C.C.'s company. The cat was all friends today, blithely oblivious to his role in last night's fiasco. He wound around her legs, tail a silky flag, purr rumbling cheerfully.

Then, while she was holding the cat on the far side of the stables and trying to decide what she wanted to do next, she saw something that gave her a small jolt of guilt. Mike was out there working in the pouring rain, sawing up the downed tree that Barry had mentioned last night when she demanded fuel for the fireplaces. Barry himself was nowhere to be seen. He was no doubt warm and dry somewhere, having sent Mike out to do the dirty work. Some of her hostility toward Mike evaporated as she watched him swinging the ax to split the big chunks of wood. On sudden impulse she set the cat down and cut through the trees toward Mike.

She was certain he was aware of her approach, but he ignored her completely. He swung the ax as if he had a grudge against the log, although she suspected his real hostility was against her. When he paused to rest for a moment, foot braced against the back bumper of an old truck, she said, "I could throw the wood into the truck for you."

He turned to look at her, blue eyes chilly as the swimming pool. "It's not your responsibility."

"I'd really like to help."

His shoulders moved within the yellow slicker in an unfriendly, suit-yourself gesture. She started throwing the split chunks of wood into the truck. She worked steadily, sometimes climbing into the truck to rearrange the chunks and make more room, until he finally paused in his chopping and offered a grudging compliment.

"You're a pretty good wood loader." When she didn't stop work, he said, "You can take a break once in a while, you know."

She stopped work, grateful for the rest, but determinedly didn't let him know that throwing the wood into the truck was taking its toll on her shoulders and back.

"I hear the baron is having dinner with you tonight," Mike added.

Lynn eyed him warily, wondering what else he had heard from Barry. On second thought, however, she doubted that Barry was announcing the fact that his seduction efforts had been rewarded with a splash of cold coffee in the anatomical area men generally considered their greatest pride and joy. Yet Mike did act a little wary himself, even a bit jumpy, as if he weren't certain about her intentions with the sticks of wood she was tossing around.

"I hope he shows up," Lynn said, although at the moment she was having some second thoughts about that. Her demand for firewood had sent Mike out here to work in the rain; she didn't like to think that her demand to see the baron might get him up out of a sickbed and perhaps even make his condition worse. When Mike offered no comment on the baron, Lynn added, "What's happened to Tristan? My roommate is disappointed that he hasn't been around."

"Am I supposed to be Tristan's keeper?" Mike flared. He sounded grumpy and out of sorts, for which Lynn could hardly blame him. Every time he bent over to whack the ax into a chunk of wood, rain hit him on the back of the neck and trickled inside his shirt.

"The rooms really are awfully cold," she said during another pause, by way of apology for putting him through this. "I really appreciate your getting the wood for us today."

Lynn thought surely there would be some efficient and relatively easy way to get the wood up to the rooms, but there wasn't. They had to carry the sticks up an armload at a time. "Isn't there a better way to do this?" she panted, after yet another climb up the circular staircase. "How did they do it in the old days?"

"Servants," Mike said with succinct brevity. "But servants aren't a dime a dozen these days, as they were back then."

Lynn pointed out her own room when they were delivering firewood to it. Apparently Barry had mentioned to him the maid's observation about heavy bedroom traffic because he looked around as if expecting to find masculine shoes under the bed.

"Melody and I share the room, as I believe I've mentioned before." Although why she was bothering to make this point clear to him, she didn't know. She didn't care if he thought she slept with a different male guest every night, she thought defiantly.

"Tristan wants to see Melody," Mike said rather abruptly. "He'll be in touch with her."

Lynn wasn't sure that was really good news for Melody, but she said, "I'll tell her." She rushed on before she had time to think about what she was going to say and change her mind. "Mike, if I unfairly accused you of something yesterday, I'm sorry. It was just that Melody said Tristan did ask about me, and I assumed he passed the information along to you. But if that wasn't true—"

Mike wiped the mixture of rain and sweat off his face with the back of his hand. He was carrying armloads of wood twice as large as Lynn's. Rain had plastered his dark hair to his head. He neither affirmed nor denied having discussed her with Tristan.

Finally he scowled and said, "It's..." His voice trailed off and Lynn filled in the word for him.

"I know. Complicated."

Everyone dressed more formally than usual and gathered expectantly before dinner to await the baron's arrival. Lynn wore a dark skirt and silky, cream-colored blouse with a femininely ruffled neckline. She was looking forward to meeting the baron, but she was not feeling particularly vivacious. Her muscles ached from all the wood carrying she'd done that day. She'd intended to take a soothing hot bath, but the hot water was gone by the time she got her turn in the bathroom. She still half expected that the baron wouldn't show up, that Barry would arrive with excuses instead, but there was no mistaking the baron when he walked in.

He looked exactly as she had expected. Thick, silvery hair, a bit rumpled, lively mustache to match, beaming smile. His jacket was the tartan plaid of Tristan's kilt, but he wore dark slacks rather than a kilt below it. His eyes were still the incredible MacNorris blue, unfaded by age, although his back was not as straight as the younger men's, and his skin had a ruddy, weathered roughness of age.

Lynn stepped forward to greet him warmly. "Baron MacNorris! It's a real pleasure to finally meet you. I'm Lynn Marquet. I talked with you briefly on the phone sometime back. I hope you're feeling better? Barry said you'd been ill."

She put out her hand, then wished she hadn't, afraid perhaps that wasn't proper etiquette with a baron. He took the hand and shook it warmly, however. He had a good, firm grip, stronger than she expected. He looked hearty enough, but he pointed to his throat and shook his head regretfully.

"You're still having trouble with the laryngitis?" Lynn asked sympathetically.

He nodded and tried to say something, but it came out an unintelligible croak. She patted his shoulder. "You don't need to say a word. We're just glad you came. I'll let everyone introduce themselves."

People filed by to shake hands with the baron, surprising Lynn by acting like normal, polite adults in civilized society. No one said or did anything peculiar or outrageous; Mark didn't bring his rat to dinner; Chris and Christy acted like a nice young married couple; Reva didn't skulk around taking notes. No one asked ridiculous or too-personal questions.

Lynn was also surprised that the baron had come alone. Considering his laryngitis, she'd have thought Barry would come along to help. The omission seemed inconsiderate, to say the least. But Barry had never been noted for his thoughtfulness, she suspected. And the dinner was probably more congenial without his disapproving presence.

The cook caught her eye from the doorway. When Lynn hurried over, the cook informed her that there was still no waitress.

This was as good a time as any to let the baron in on the problems they were encountering at the castle, Lynn decided. She'd explain things to him in an offhand way and let him take it from there. He'd been quick enough to straighten

Barry out on the phone; he'd no doubt do it again, perhaps even more forcefully, once he realized the extent of the castle's deficiencies. Perhaps that was why Barry had discreetly decided to stay away tonight. He'd probably rather take his dressing down in private.

"I'm afraid I'll have to excuse myself," she said when she returned to the baron. "It appears the girl who was working as maid and waitress quit and a replacement hasn't been hired, so my roommate and I have been filling in."

She waited for him to make some expression of surprise or indignation, but he merely nodded approvingly and patted her shoulder. He croaked something that might have been, "Good lass," before turning away to toss another peppermint at one of the women.

Well, subtlety hadn't worked, she realized regretfully. She'd have to be more direct with complaints to him after dinner.

The meal and socializing afterward went nicely. In spite of the baron's inability to add anything vocal to the conversation, there was more conversation than usual, and none of the usual snapping and grumbling. The baron flirted wordlessly with the women and had an easy camaraderie with the men. He exuded a cheerful good humor that enlivened the whole atmosphere, and he was completely devoid of any air of snobbish aloofness or superiority because of his status as a baron.

Baron MacNorris was, in fact, something of a bumbler. He sloshed his tea, stumbled over a chair leg, got sauce on his mustache and knocked a figurine off the mantel. And each time he'd just grin apologetically and fumble ineptly trying to make amends, in the process managing to endear himself to everyone.

Once, passing Lynn sitting on a sofa, he tossed one of his trademark peppermints to her, as he had been doing with all the women. Her peppermint, however, landed neatly in the oval of her ruffled neckline, and she had to reach inside and fish it out from between her breasts. If it had been any other man, she'd have suspected the peppermint had been deliberately aimed to drop into her cleavage, but the old baron wouldn't do that, of course. It was just poor aim, more of his innocent bumbling. She smiled at him as she put the peppermint in her mouth.

Regretfully, however, she decided she must get him off to one side and talk to him. He came willingly when she said she'd like to speak with him for a moment about a problem. But when they got to a corner of the room he had a terrible coughing attack and had to sit down. His hand shook as he put a peppermint in his mouth.

It was then she realized she couldn't possibly burden this sweet, bumbling, unwell old man with castle problems. It was Barry's responsibility to take care of things and she would simply have to insist he correct the deficiencies or make a considerable reduction in the rates. She should never have demanded to see the baron, knowing he hadn't been well, although she was glad he'd come to dinner.

"You just sit right there, and I'll get you a glass of water," she said solicitously as he took a deep breath between coughs. "By the way, where is Barry tonight?"

The baron pantomimed the bent head and scribbling hand of someone engrossed in bookkeeping or correspondence. She got the water for him and then slipped out as Reva decided to let him in on the marvelous fact that she was writing a book with his Scottish castle as a background.

Lynn hurried over to the cottage. Light shone dimly through the closed curtains. She rang the bell, but there was no answer. She rang it several more times, aware that she needn't worry about disturbing the baron now. Finally she opened the door a crack.

A yellow blur at her feet was Castle Cat, who must have been lurking in the shadows waiting for just such an opportunity to streak inside. He jumped on the desk and purred as if they were old friends.

Except for the cat, the room was empty. She decided there was no point in acting mousy about this. "Barry?" she called assertively. "Are you here?"

Again, no answer. She smiled a bit grimly. Barry apparently was not as hard at work as the old baron innocently believed. She called again. The only answer was a meow from Castle Cat when she stopped petting him for a moment.

On sudden impulse Lynn stepped around to the far side of the desk. It was none of her business, of course, but what *were* all these papers cluttering Barry's desk? She noted that this time there was no leftover half cup of cold coffee; perhaps Barry had learned a lesson from last night's incident.

The clutter included letters from prospective guests, lists of what appeared to be castle antiques, letters and pamphlets about various swimming-pool heating systems, catalogs and travel magazines. But mostly there were bills. Bills, bills and more bills, many with angry notations about overdue amounts.

Lynn had just picked up a letter with the elegant imprint of a legal firm when she saw Castle Cat look toward the door. A moment later she heard what the cat's sharp ears had caught before she did, the sound of footsteps on the stone doorstep.

The baron returning—or Barry? Whoever it was, the last thing she wanted was to be caught going through private papers like a common snoop! She should never have given into such an unforgivable impulse.

She glanced around in panic and then dived for the hallway and the nearest open door.

The room was unlit. Lynn could see nothing, only hear the clicks of the outside door opening and closing. She held her arms close to her rigid body, hardly daring to breathe, afraid she might touch something and make some incriminating noise.

"Hey, C.C., what're you doing in here? You're supposed to be out catching castle mice."

She puzzled over the voice, realizing in surprise that Barry and Mike sounded so much alike that she couldn't tell which of them it was. On second thought, however, she knew it had to be Mike. Barry would never have spoken so affectionately to the cat.

She relaxed slightly. Mike must merely have stopped by the cottage to see Barry for a minute. When he discovered Barry wasn't there he'd leave, and then she could escape before Barry or the baron returned.

She expected Mike to call for Barry, as she had done, but there were only more murmurs as he carried on a casual conversation with the cat. Then, to her dismay, she heard the conversation moving down the hallway. The action puzzled her, but she hadn't time to reflect on it; the idea of being caught skulking around the cottage was as bad as being found snooping in private papers.

She retreated farther into the room so he couldn't see her when he passed the doorway, and then in panic she realized he wasn't passing by. His big silhouette filled the open doorway. Her only good fortune was that by then her eyes had adjusted to the dim light and she could see another open door at one side of the room. She lunged into the opening just before the light went on.

She was immediately tangled in clothes hanging from the rod and shoes and various other unidentifiable objects underfoot. She thought surely he must hear her threshing around, but he was still talking to the cat. Finally she got herself braced against one wall, hands damp with nervous perspiration. She carefully took shallow, silent breaths and wondered frantically if she was going to start some giveaway hiccuping or sneezing.

There was then total silence outside her cramped quarters, silence that was somehow unnerving because she was certain he hadn't left the room. What could he be doing?

Perhaps Mike also was involved in a bit of opportune snooping? Curiosity got the better of her, and she cautiously moved her head enough to peer out the open door.

What she saw was enough to make her wonder if her ears
and eyes were playing tricks on her, because it was neither
Mike nor Barry that she saw. It was the baron. He had taken
off his jacket and was standing at a dressing table, leaning
forward to examine his reflection in the big mirror. He
seemed taller, less stooped with age.

But the surprise of seeing that it was the baron in the
room was nothing compared to the next surprise. Because
what he did next was to reach up and peel off the mustache. He set it carefully on the dressing table. And then he
removed the aristocratic, silvery-gray hair and set it behind
the mustache. He spoke to the two phony pieces, which
somehow held the essence of the baron image, as if they
were human.

"Well, old boy, you did pretty well for yourself this evening, if I do say so myself." He gave the wig an affection-
ate pat. And, incredibly, at the other end of the dressing
table were another wig and mustache, blond.

Lynn must have made some unintentional noise of astonishment, because ever-alert Castle Cat suddenly looked
her way. Lynn instantly ducked her head back into the
closet, but it was the wrong action. The metal hangers rattled noisily when she collided with them. She held her breath
as footsteps approached softly.

She closed her eyes, as if with that childhood gesture she
could shut out everything and keep it from happening. Her
mind reeled with the peculiarities of the situation. She felt
as if she'd stumbled into some Scottish corner of *The Twilight Zone*. Barry was pretending to be the baron? *Why?* But
it had been Mike's voice she had heard talking to Castle
Cat…and that was unmistakably Tristan's rough blond hair
on the dressing table.

The clothes hangers skidded along the wooden rod as a
strong arm swept them aside. Lynn reluctantly opened her
eyes. A MacNorris male was looking at her. But *which*
MacNorris male, she was dizzily uncertain. The skin looked
lined and rough, the baron's skin. The hair, rumpled when

the wig was removed, was Mike's, the brown color a youthful contrast to the silver-gray eyebrows below. The voice, which now spoke to her in frosty tones, held Barry's aloof superiority.

"Ah, the lady of the night strikes once more. Were you looking for something you didn't find in the garbage cans? Or perhaps planning to wait until I was asleep and then pounce on me in the dark with more cold coffee?"

"Barry?" she said doubtfully. Only the eyes was she certain of. They were MacNorris blue all the way.

"Sometimes," he said. It came out sounding more like a sigh of resignation than a word. He motioned toward a nightstand, where Lynn now saw, like another stray piece of someone she knew, a familiar pair of heavy, dark-rimmed glasses.

She stepped out of the closet. "Why are you impersonating the baron?" she demanded. "And who...who *are* you?"

"I'm not impersonating the baron. I am the baron."

Lynn shook her head, dazed, as she fell farther into this weird new world where everything was askew. The room looked normal enough. Big, four-postered bed with fluffy down comforter, well-worn chairs that looked more just plain old than antique, wall poster of Garfield the cat giving some droll advice, pile of dirty work clothes by the bed.

But on the dressing table were those...those bits of other people.

"I'm also Mike—" Blaze of boyish grin, snapped on and off as if a switch were flipped. He reached into the closet and brought out a familiar tartan-plaid kilt. "And your trusty chauffeur Tristan, as well."

Lynn shook her head again in bewilderment. "I don't understand."

"Well, as I told you, it's complicated." He took off his shirt and walked over to the dressing table. He picked up a jar and started applying a cream to his skin. The baron's rough, ruddy complexion came off on the cloth when he wiped his face. He leaned over and brushed away the powder that grayed his eyebrows.

Lynn watched with a kind of morbid fascination. It wasn't exactly a Dr.-Jekyll-and-Mr.-Hyde transformation, but seeing the familiar face of Barry—or was it Mike?—emerge from under the makeup was disconcerting.

Unexpectedly he laughed, his eyes meeting her reflection in the mirror with honest amusement. "You needn't look so wide-eyed. I'm not some dangerous psycho with multiple, deviant personalities, who goes around hacking up castle guests with antique cutlery."

He turned to face her. She jumped when he put his hands on her shoulders, but he didn't let go.

"I wanted to tell you, Lynn. Honestly I did. I started to, several times. I really intended to when you came back after we went to the ruins, because I was afraid if I didn't, we'd lose out on something special with each other. But then you started making all those wild accusations about Tristan and me and female guests who were 'ripe for plucking.' And then I was going to tell you last night, but you dumped coffee on me before I had a chance, and—"

Lynn dropped to the edge of the bed. This weird new world was some sort of crazy kaleidoscope and every few moments a giant force shook the pieces into some new and confusing pattern. Nothing was fixed or dependable.

"You're telling me that you're *everyone*?" she finally asked a little faintly.

He nodded. "Everyone. Barry, Mike, Tristan. And the baron, too, of course."

"What about the cook and the maid?" Lynn asked, studying him with suspicion as she remembered the maid being in her room once when she was in nothing but bra and bikini panties. His masculine body hardly looked as if it would have fit into the maid's dress, but at the moment anything seemed possible.

He laughed and shook his head. "No, I'm not the cook or the maid, although if I could have figured out a way to pull it off I probably would have been. But even an actor with padding and a dress can't fake cooking believably."

"You really are an actor, then?" Lynn asked. "That much was true?"

He nodded. "Actually, almost everything was true, more or less. It was just that I kind of split and rearranged facts. I'm sorry, Lynn, I really am. I never really intended to deceive you—"

"You can hardly expect me to believe that the whole charade was accidental!"

"No, of course not. So I guess I did intend to deceive you at first, but then I met you, and—" he shook his head a little helplessly. "You're upset, aren't you?"

Lynn folded her arms across her chest. Yes, she was upset, and it was more than the simple fact of his deceiving her with the multiple personalities. She felt as if her *emotions* had been deceived, that he'd unfairly played with them.

"Suppose you start way back at the beginning, wherever that might be, and tell me what this is really all about," she said. "For starters, who *are* you?"

"I'm Baron Conor Michael Barry MacNorris. I got stuck with Conor because that was the old baron's name, and my parents wanted to get in his good graces by naming me after him. But they then couldn't agree on a middle name, so I got both Michael and Barry. And then I just sort of...split the names into individual personalities and used them." He gave her a Mike smile, a little lopsided, as if hoping she would take it all as just good, innocent fun.

She refused to do that. "What about Tristan?"

"Tristan, I must admit, was pure invention. I thought it was a rather romantic sounding name that would appeal to American guests."

"But . . . but none of this makes sense!" Lynn protested, feeling more confused than ever as her memory tossed out conflicting details. "Barry was so *critical* of Mike, accusing him of not attending to business, of sneaking off to hunt for secret passageways or explore old ruins. And Mike was so *gleeful* about frustrating Barry...and scornful of Tristan's superstud masculinity.''

"That's true. Mike and Barry tend to do those things. Mike gets fed up with old nose-to-the-grindstone Barry, and he does skip off to go exploring and have a little fun. That irresponsible attitude really frustrates Barry, of course, who believes in work, work, work. And they both think Tristan carries that macho undress-'em-with-his-eyes, love-'em-and-leave-'em attitude a bit too far.'' He spoke seriously, as if he were discussing a trio of good, if flawed, friends.

"But you're Barry! And Mike—and Tristan, too!''

He grinned engagingly. "I told you. It's complicated.''

"The beginning,'' Lynn insisted. "The very beginning.''

Chapter Seven

Okay," he agreed. "But this is going to take a while, so you may as well make yourself comfortable."

He followed the suggestion himself. He kicked off his shoes, reached to the head of the bed and tossed her a pillow. He pounded the other pillow into a suitable shape, stuffed it under his head and stretched out on his side of the bed.

After a moment's hesitation she carefully lay down on her stomach, chin propped in her hands, but she kept a cautious distance between herself and him. A Mike-Barry-Tristan combination could well be as dangerous as dynamite with a lit fuse, she suspected. She'd been attracted to each of them individually—as well as furious with each of them individually—and now here they were rolled up into one man. It was a dizzying thought.

Something else suddenly occurred to her. She sat up abruptly, feet hitting the floor with a thud. Sore muscles in her back and shoulders screeched protest at the sudden movement, but she ignored them.

"That was no accident when you—you the *baron*—threw the peppermint down the front of my blouse this evening," she accused indignantly. "You did it on purpose."

He grinned guilty acknowledgement. "I figured a bumbling old baron could get away with something like that. Although what I really wanted to do was—"

He eyed the blouse as if he were boldly considering carrying out "the baron's" earlier thoughts. Lynn didn't inquire what those thoughts were, but the dangerous glint in his eyes made her slap a protective hand over the ruffled neckline of the blouse. Tristan, she suspected, was quite capable of a swashbuckling bodice rip. And this *was* Tristan lying here beside her, even though his blond hair and mustache were over on the dresser. She felt a little dizzy again as she looked into the blue eyes on the opposite pillow. Mike-Barry-Tristan-the Baron. How could she possibly cope with all of them melded into one body? One very attractive body...

"I looked for you before I left the castle, you know," he added. "I wondered what had become of you."

"Now you know what became of me. I was over here hiding in your closet. Stop changing the subject."

"And that reminds me. I'm sure there is some perfectly logical reason you were hiding in my closet, but merely out of curiosity, just *why*—"

She had started to lie down again, but when she sat up so abruptly she'd jerked an already sore muscle in her back and now she winced as she moved.

"What's wrong?" he asked.

"I guess I'm not accustomed to carrying a tree, even one split into pieces, into a castle," she admitted.

He got up and moved around behind her. "Where does it hurt? Here?" He lightly massaged the muscles along the ridge of her shoulder. "Here?" His fingers ran down the long muscles beside her spine.

Lynn nodded at each place his finger probed. "It hurts everywhere," she said, although along with the pain went a much different, very pleasurable awareness of his touch. He had an appealing scent of some tweedy male cologne, very Scottish baronish. "I was planning to take a long hot soak in the bathtub, but there wasn't enough hot water. Which is another often-voiced complaint among the guests that I intended to bring to the baron's attention."

"The baron is well aware of all the problems. Look, how about soaking in the bathtub here for a while?" When she looked shocked at the suggestion, he held up one hand in solemn oath. "I swear, I won't try to jump in with you. Unless invited, of course."

She wasn't convinced. "How many of you are swearing to that?" In spite of knowing that the man with her was everyone, she still halfway expected to see some other MacNorris male stroll through the doorway.

"All of us. On our Scout's honor."

Lynn had her doubts about the propriety of taking a bath in these circumstances, but she knew the hot water would again be gone by the time she got back to the castle, and the prospect of soothing her sore muscles in a hot soak was too tempting to resist.

He showed her to the bathroom down the hall. It, like the castle bathrooms, had a tub that was much deeper and narrower than those back home, and the faucets had huge, fan-shaped brass handles with an ornate pattern of swirls and loops. He brought towels, washcloth and soap for her.

"And if you need your back washed—"

"Thank you, but I've been washing my own back for a number of years and I'm sure I can manage to do it now," she answered tartly.

The door had an old-fashioned bolt, and she locked it securely behind him when he went out. When she didn't hear any departing footsteps, she asked, "What are you doing?"

"Standing guard."

"I really don't think that's necessary. There are only the two of us here."

Silence from the other side of the door as they both contemplated the dubious reliability of the four-in-one personality of one of those present.

She heard the sound of a chair scraping the floor as he pulled it up to sit by the door. She checked the door again. Securely locked. No keyhole. Even Tristan would surely be thwarted by such barriers.

He started his story while she was undressing. She hung her skirt and blouse on a hook on the door. Until that moment she hadn't realized that Castle Cat had somehow gotten into the bathroom with her. He regarded her with lazy golden eyes, like some aristocrat temporarily ensconced in cat disguise.

"First of all, there was the old baron, Baron Conor MacNorris. He was my grandfather's brother. He was married once, but they never had children and his wife died some years ago. The old baron and my father didn't get along at all, but my parents shipped me over for a couple of summer visits, with the not-too-subtle plot in mind that I would so ingratiate myself with the baron that he would leave everything to me. It was, I might add, practically the only thing they ever agreed on about me or anything else."

Lynn paused in the act of unfastening her sheer black nylons from the lacy black garter belt.

"Tristan's parents." Lynn faced the door in sudden realization. "You told me about Tristan's parents who stuck together and made themselves and everyone around them miserable. These were *your* parents."

"I am Tristan, and Tristan is me. Therefore, you are correct. Our parents are one and the same." He spoke gravely, as if it were some complicated mathematical problem they had just solved together.

"This is *very* confusing," Lynn said reprovingly. She draped the garter belt on the hook with the other clothes but left the nylons on the floor. "Wait a minute, now, until I run some water in the tub."

While the tub was filling she shimmied out of her lacy black panties. She had never been able to explain it even to herself, but while she tended to select mostly conservative outergarments, she'd always had a weakness for frothy underthings. She sank luxuriously into the half-full tub of hot water, sorry only that she hadn't any bubble bath. She told him to go on.

"Anyway, surprisingly enough, their plot worked. The old baron became quite fond of me, as I was of him, and we carried on a now-and-then correspondence. He had other relatives, grandchildren of his two sisters, but none of them had the MacNorris name, to which he had a powerful sentimental attachment. So in his will he merely left them some ugly old cash, and I, the only member of the family who still had the grand and glorious family name, *I* got the big prize, the castle and the title."

"Were the others angry?"

"I think perhaps they were at first. But then they, and I, realized that there were some drawbacks to my marvelous inheritance."

"Which were?"

He interjected an aside comment. "I'd like to point out that I wasn't trying to deceive anyone by presenting myself as the baron, although I did ... ah ... advance my age a bit. But I really am the baron. According to the hearthstone, anyway."

"Okay, you really are a baron," Lynn conceded. An unlikely baron, but apparently a baron nevertheless. There was an oddly intimate feeling to being naked in the hot water, with only a door separating her from him as they talked. Her mind wandered a bit. Suppose she did ask him to come in and wash her back.... There was something deliciously enticing about the thought, even as she instantly rejected it and hastily said, "But I don't understand what the catch was."

"There were enormous death taxes on the estate. And, even more shocking, I soon also learned the castle was heavily mortgaged. Somehow you don't think of timeless old castles as being unpaid for—at least I didn't—but the old baron had borrowed heavily against this one. It seems he had this one wee character flaw. He liked to dash off to Monte Carlo and gamble. The castle roof was in a terrible state of disrepair and had to be worked on immediately, and then the plumbing did strange things. As soon as I fixed one thing, something else fell apart. And insurance!" He groaned. "Have you any idea how much it costs to insure a castle? Anyway, all this involved money, lots of it, and I didn't have any, of course, because the other heirs got what cash there was."

"You could have liquidated everything, grabbed whatever was left after the debts were taken care of and run," she pointed out.

"Or just thrown up my hands and run without all the preliminary hassles, because there probably wouldn't have been much to grab."

"But you couldn't do that. Because the old baron had left it to you trusting that it would remain in MacNorris hands, that there would be a Baron MacNorris. Noblesse oblige."

"Nobility obligates is putting it a bit melodramatically, but I did feel obliged to do what I could with the place."

"And you're not without a certain affection for it," Lynn added thoughtfully.

"I decided the only possible solution was to make the castle somehow pay its own way. Hence the rent-a-castle scheme. What are you doing?" he asked unexpectedly.

What she was doing was drawing whimsical soapsuds faces around her navel, but she wasn't about to tell him that, of course. "Just soaking. But I still don't see how all this translates into becoming Mike-Barry-Tristan, and an elderly baron, as well. By the way, since that name is a bit difficult to handle, what do you prefer to be called?"

"Do you really intend to call me anything after all this?" He sounded almost wistful.

She was beginning to sympathize with Mike-Barry-Tristan's problems, but she didn't understand everything yet and wasn't about to make promises at this point. "I'll think about it," she said warily.

"Before I became a baron, I was just plain Mike Mac-Norris." Wryly he added, "I think that was because another of the many things my parents couldn't agree on was how to pronounce Conor."

"Okay, Mike, suppose you explain your other personalities, then." Lynn still felt confused. She realized now why she so often couldn't locate Barry, of course; he was off being someone else at the time, sometimes even with her. It also explained teddy-bear pajamas; Barry might not be a teddy-bear sort of person, but Mike definitely was. And obviously she and Mike, and Melody and Tristan, couldn't make up a fun foursome, because Mike and Tristan were one. No wonder that suggestion had been so unequivocally rejected. Yet it was still difficult *not* to think of Mike and Barry and Tristan as separate people. She didn't feel out of *The Twilight Zone* even yet.

"Actually, you were partly to blame."

"Me?" Lynn sat up indignantly in the tub. "That's ridiculous."

"You called and woke me in the middle of the night, remember? I'd spent all day trying to get that old mower running and I was tired and grumpy. But then I woke up enough to realize I was about to lose a customer I desperately needed, so on the spur of the moment I passed myself off as a secretary and invented the nice old baron to smooth things over. I really wasn't thinking any further ahead than that. If I had thought ahead, perhaps I'd have seen I was taking the first dangerous step into one very large pit of castle quicksand, in which I've been floundering ever since."

Lynn thought back to that night. "But I distinctly heard two people talking."

"I used to do a hand puppet show for kids when I was in college. My left hand was Herman the Owl and my right was

Otto the Woodpecker. Herman and Otto would get into these screeching, pecking fights, you see..."

Lynn saw what he was getting at. Doing a Scottish baron and an American secretary talking to each other wasn't a challenge for a man who could do an owl and a woodpecker in an argument. She slid back into the water again. Her sore muscles were feeling much better now. She ran her foot over the fanciful metalwork on the faucet handle, idly wondering if the swirls represented some clan insignia or were merely a graceful pattern. Castle Cat, stretched out like a fat orange rug beside the tub, purred contentedly.

"So when did your personalities split off and become whole people in the flesh?" she asked.

"About the time I realized I couldn't scrape up enough money to hire real people to staff the place. I figured if I could just get through this first group of guests that I'd be able to finance a real staff for the next guests. I'd already created a secretary and an old baron, of course, so it was simple enough to add Tristan the chauffeur and send him off to meet you. And then he, because he was Barry the secretary inside—I told you this was complicated—was appalled when he saw how many there were in the group."

Lynn nodded guiltily. No wonder Tristan had appeared so hostile. She'd suspected right from the start that the merry group she'd assembled wasn't exactly what was expected here, and her self-righteous rationalization that the secretary should have asked how many were coming was hardly a solid defense.

"So Tristan and Barry were both angry with you and worried about the financial effects of the mob invasion, too. But underneath their anger was this part of me that was very much attracted to you and wanted to get to know you and be with you. And since I still had a name and personality to spare...?" The explanation ended on a questioning note of appeal.

"So Mike the handyman-gardener came into being." Lynn shook her head, still feeling as if she were in a kaleidoscope. "But Mike said Barry's insistence that he pretend to be a native Scot was silly...."

"One part of me thought a Scottish staff would make a better impression on guests. Another part thought that was a really dumb idea." He stopped short. She could hear his fingers tapping the chair. "Sometimes, when I was using one of the names, the part of my personality that went with that name just kind of took over." Another pause. "That does sound pretty weird, doesn't it?"

Something else was also rather weird. Lynn's big toe had slipped into a swirled loop on one of the ornate faucet handles and wouldn't come out.

Of course it *would* come out, she assured herself. After all, the toe had gone into the opening, so it would surely come out the same way. She pulled gently, but all that accomplished was to slide her bare bottom along the bottom of the slick tub. She gave a good jerk with her leg.

"Ouch!"

"What did you say?" Mike asked.

"Nothing." She squirmed the toe back and forth in what seemed to be a shrinking opening. "The water feels great on my sore muscles. I really appreciate your letting me do this."

"Anytime."

By now, with the jerking and squirming, the toe was beginning to get sore. And the next thing that would happen, she realized in dismay, was that the toe would swell, and then she'd really be in a ridiculous predicament.

The thing to do, she decided, was simply put a little soap on the toe, as you would soap a finger to take off a too-tight ring, and it would slip right out.

Except, peculiar as it might seem, she couldn't reach her toe. There was something about the angles of trapped toe, ankle and knee that kept her from bending far enough to get her hands on the faucet.

"Everything okay in there?" Mike asked.

"Of course."

"You're doing a lot of splashing."

"I like to splash." An odd statement, but what else was there to say?

She regarded the ornate faucet with its treacherous swirls and loops balefully. She should be grateful, she supposed, that the toe hadn't become trapped while the faucet was running full blast. At least she wasn't in imminent danger of drowning. Then she looked at her fingers, already wrinkled from the long soaking.

She could just lie here and shrivel to death.

She gritted her teeth. If she could just get her leg turned at a slightly different angle— The leg turned. Which meant the toe also turned. And the faucet. Cold water poured into the tub as if she'd just tapped a main line to the North Sea. And she still couldn't reach her toe or the faucet.

"Lynn, are you sure nothing's wrong?"

"My toe is caught," she muttered.

"I can't hear you," he yelled over the sound of running water. "Did you say something about a toe?"

The water in the tub was getting colder and deeper by the second. Already it was approaching overflow level. She had visions of it flooding bathroom, hallway, cottage. Tabloid headlines proclaiming American tourist had drowned in freak tub accident. She mumbled something evasive, but again he yelled, "What? I can't hear you."

"MY TOE IS CAUGHT IN THE FAUCET AND I CAN'T GET IT LOOSE AND I CAN'T TURN THE WATER OFF."

Moment of silence as he digested that unlikely statement. Then he tried the door. It was locked, of course.

"I'm coming in," he said.

"No—"

Too late. His shoulder hit the door like a human tank. The bolt broke loose. Lynn's clothes flew off the hook and into the tub. Water sprayed Castle Cat, and with an outraged yowl the cat shot out of the room. Lynn, with only trapped toe and leg showing over the rim of the tub, knew Mike was out there somewhere even if she couldn't see him.

"I understood there was some guarantee of privacy with your offer of the use of your bathtub," she snapped. "Perhaps I should have gotten it in writing."

Mike spoke from outside the door he had discreetly closed part way. "Do you want privacy or do you want help getting your toe loose?"

Lynn briefly considered her options, which at the moment appeared severely limited. "Just a minute," she said.

She carefully swaddled herself in the clothes that were already in the tub with her, tucking skirt and blouse around her until she was completely covered. Water overflowed the tub, creating a miniature waterfall as it cascaded over the rim.

"If you could just turn off the water," she said with the limited dignity available to a person with a toe caught in a faucet handle.

Mike stepped into the room and turned the water off. He took a wary step backward, apparently not inclined to volunteer further assistance. Lynn tentatively wiggled her toe, but it was still securely trapped.

"Perhaps if you just put a little soap on the toe...?"

Mike soaped the toe and a moment later her foot slipped free. She wanted to rub it, but she needed all her hands to keep her wet clothing in place.

"It's a good thing I got in when I did. The toe looks as if it had started to swell. Another few minutes and it would probably have taken a hacksaw to cut you loose." By then he was also thoroughly soaked from kneeling on the wet floor.

"Yes. I'm sure you saved my toe, my life and my future. Thank you. Now if you'll just please *go* so I can dress—"

"What do you intend to dress in? This?" He picked up the only item of clothing that hadn't tumbled into the tub, the lacy black garter belt, and gave it a burlesque spin around his forefinger. He didn't wait for an answer, how-

ever. "I'll see if I can find something a bit more...
ah...substantial for you to wear."

Lynn leaped out of the tub as soon as he left the room.
She couldn't lock the door, but she put all her weight against
it. When he returned she reached a hand through a barely
opened crack to accept what he had brought. It turned out
to be a man's short, terry-cloth robe, burgundy, that came
to just above her knees.

"Hand me your clothes," he said through the door she
had quickly closed.

"I will not!"

"I was merely going to hang them to dry in front of the
electric heater. Unless you prefer to dash back to the castle
in what you're wearing?"

That would surely arouse some interested speculation. She
handed the clothes out and rinsed her nylons in the sink. By
the time she got back to the bedroom, which appeared to be
his main living quarters, he had everything draped on chairs
in front of an electric heater. The lacy black panties hung
from a corner bedpost like some saucy flag flying in the
breeze created by the heater fan. She added the nylons to the
display without comment.

"I hope everything was of the washable variety?" he said.

"Fortunately, yes."

"How's the toe?"

"I don't believe there was time for gangrene to set in."

He pulled up another chair so she could sit on the pe-
riphery of the heat. A bedraggled Castle Cat, ears flattened
in disgust at his wet condition, had the choice spot right in
front of the heater. Lynn tucked the terry-cloth robe firmly
around her. Mike had changed to dry jeans and an old,
buttonless khaki shirt that hung open over his chest.

"Have I now explained everything to your satisfaction?" he inquired. Wryly he answered himself. "Perhaps
not. There are, of course, all your complaints about the
castle. I honestly didn't mean to engage in deceptive adver-
tising. It was just that nothing went as I planned. After I'd

placed the ad, something went wrong with the Rolls-Royce—"

"So it really is in the shop, as you said?"

"Not now. I couldn't pay the repair bill and had to sell it."

"And the unheated pool?"

"It never was heated, of course, when the old baron was alive. He believed fresh air and cold water built character. But I was fairly certain that Americans on vacation would prefer comfort to character building, so I bought a used heating system intending to have it ready to go by the time the first guests got here. Then, after it was installed, I discovered it wouldn't work and replacement parts weren't available, and I hadn't the money to buy a new system. Let's see, what were your other complaints?"

"Frigid rooms."

"Ah, yes, the infamous frigid rooms." He looked at her suspiciously. "I've seen those guys leering at you. Some of those looks were hot enough to warm the castle dungeon."

"But they haven't been warming my bedroom," she answered with an if-it's-any-of-your-business tartness.

He made some noncommittal sound and returned to the subject of castle complaints. "What I told you about figuring it would be warmer by now was the truth. I thought I could get by without buying coal for the fireplaces. Who'd have guessed it was going to rain the whole damned time," he added sourly.

"There are also the troutless trout ponds," she reminded.

"An honest mistake on my part. I thought there were trout in them because I caught fish there when I was here as a kid. I didn't realize the ponds had to be restocked occasionally. And, of course, when I did realize it I hadn't the money to do it."

"And the missing furniture and antiques?"

"Sold. I've been scraping up money wherever I could. But I haven't had enough to upgrade the hot-water heating system or to add more bathrooms. You must admit, however, that the missing maid wasn't really my fault," he added, managing to inject a virtuous note into the statement. "And the wine from the old baron's wine cellar has been first-rate."

"That's true," Lynn agreed. "Everyone has been very happy with the wine. And I'm sorry Spike scared off the maid. He really is quite harmless, you know." Her knees were getting too warm, and she stood up to turn her backside to the heater. The cottage was cold, and trying to keep warm with the heater was rather like sitting around a campfire.

"There was one little thing I didn't tell you. When the maid quit, she included me in her 'crazy Americans' accusation. I had to let the maid and the cook in on my scheme, of course, and both of them have been a bit...ah...alarmed by my multiple personalities."

"Perhaps not an unreasonable attitude," Lynn murmured. She looked at him curiously. "How much of those personalities was invention, and how much is really you?"

"I guess they're all part of me," he answered, not sounding too happy about the admission. "Tristan is long on old-fashioned male chauvinism, short on commitment. He's the sweep-her-off-her-feet type."

"I thought of him as the Scottish superstud," Lynn agreed.

He laughed ruefully and then tilted his head to look at her speculatively. "But you were interested in him."

Lynn didn't commit herself, but that was true. She stretched a foot out to stroke Castle Cat with her toe. His yellow-orange fur was regaining its normal fluff, although he wasn't in a good enough humor to purr yet.

"Mike is the irresponsible kid in me who never quite grew up. And Barry is the conscience, I suppose, always disapproving of the things that other less practical and sensible parts of me want to do. He keeps me in line. Most of the time, anyway." He rearranged her skirt hanging on the back of a chair so it would dry more evenly. "When I start examining me in parts, I'm not too thrilled with what I see."

One part superstud, one part small boy, one part conscience. Plus a few minor parts he hadn't separated out and named, Lynn suspected. Yet she liked what it all added up to, like a recipe with separate ingredients that individually sound questionable adding up to a fantastic dish.

"And what about that sweet, bumbling old baron?" Lynn asked. "Where does he fit in?"

Mike lifted one shoulder and shook his head. "Maybe the baron is me in another thirty-five or forty years." He came over to stand by her. He touched her lightly under the chin and tilted her head up. "How does that strike you?"

The tiny MacNorris mole on his cheek was plainly visible when she looked up at him. She brushed a fingertip across the skin above his upper lip, realizing now that the faint reddish mark was a souvenir of mustaches zipped on and off. Yes, the old baron who had come to dinner could be Mike in thirty or forty years, sweet and charming and mischievously sexy.

"Will he still be carrying peppermints and tossing them into inappropriate places?"

Mike grinned. "I have no doubt about it. His aim may falter a bit with age, but never his lusty intentions."

They looked at each other for a long moment, each of them realizing that they had wandered into deeper water here. The future. Yet the only future they really had was what remained of this week.

His hands slid to her waist and pulled her toward him with gentle insistence. She knew what he was thinking. It was in the smolder of his eyes, the pressure of his hands. Last night he'd asked her to stay with him. He was wordlessly asking it again now.

And one part of her was saying *no*, and another part was recklessly countering, *why not?* Time was so short....

Yet if she did do what he was silently asking, and the feelings inside her blossomed into the love that she knew was budding there, what then? Perhaps she knew him almost too well, she thought ruefully. In his multiple personalities he had revealed more of himself to her than most men would in the length of time they had known each other. There was so much of him she could fall in love with. But he was a man who had warned her that the Tristan part of him dodged commitment and couldn't be trusted.

Yet she'd tried commitment herself once and it hadn't been the secure fortress she'd thought it would be.

"You still think I'm kind of crazy, don't you?" Mike said with a sigh.

"How reliable is the judgment of a woman who falls off a pile of garbage cans and gets her toe caught in a faucet handle?" she asked lightly. She'd always thought of herself as, if not graceful, at least dignified, but she seemed to be turning into a confirmed klutz.

He jumped on the implication of the question. "Then you *do* think I'm a certified case of weirdo multiple personalities. Destined to become case number forty-two in some psychiatric textbook. Or the subject of next year's psycho-thriller movie. *The Split Baron of Norbrae*, the movie that asks the terrifying question: if personality A and personality B can't get along, will they cut the castle in two with a chain saw?"

"Well . . ." she hedged.

"Do you honestly think I'm so different from everyone else?" he asked, his tone turning more serious. "Don't you think everyone has these little parts of character that carry on guerrilla skirmishes with other parts? One part that wants to goof off and another that nags you into going off to work every day? One that says *save* while another says *spend*? One part that yearns for home and marriage—and another that would blithely like to flit from the arms of one sexy partner to another? It was just that I split my character parts off and made them into full-blown, walking, talking people." He stopped short as if reconsidering what he'd just said. He ran a hand through his dark hair and turned away from her. "That really does sound crazy, doesn't it?"

"Oh, I don't know...."

Lynn was suddenly thinking about herself, her own sometimes ill-fitting facets of character. She had never separated them into compartments, but they were there. There was the part that budgeted her earnings carefully, prudently saving for a rainy day, buying sensible shoes on sale. And there was another reckless part, the part that bought lacy black garter belts and sexy panties and teddies, the same part that occasionally grabbed control and said, *Oh, the hell with being sensible. Let's buy that slinky black velvet dress and those sky-high heels to go with it, too.*

There was the part of her that said *Dump this dull job. Figure out what you really want and go for it.* To be immediately pounced on by the part that demanded *security* at any price. There was the part of her that loved babies, small animals and sentimental movies... and the part that had bumped and swayed with sensuous abandon through belly-dancing lessons. The old-fashioned part that looked doubtfully on carefree intimacies and the part that shamelessly considered carrying on tempestuous vacation affairs with two men at the same time. Although the odd thing was that the only time that thought had ever occurred to her, the two men had turned out to be the same man!

She might even give names to the conflicting facets of personality. Miss Prudence, cool and prim, competent, dependable and dull, easily shocked. Nancy, all-American nice girl, eternally cheerful, conventional as apple pie and vanilla ice cream, everybody's small-town girl next door. And Tanya the Temperamental Temptress, usually safely locked in some dark mental closet, but wild as a barefoot gypsy when she sneaked out.

Tanya the Temptress grabbed hold now. Lynn reached up and touched Mike on the back of the neck. Her fingertips made whispery circles on his skin and adventured into his hair. If they had only a few more days—and nights—why not make the most of them?

Chapter Eight

He turned and took her in his arms, instantly catching the change in her from wary to reckless.

"Lynn..." The name that had always sounded so cool and controlled suddenly became, in Mike's husky tones, an invocation of desire and passion.

She didn't speak, just lifted her mouth to his. They met as equals in desire, lips lingering in a long kiss that gave sensuous physical expression to each of the male personalities that had intrigued her. The kiss had Tristan's scorching fire, Barry's hidden passions, Mike's lighthearted teasing. She returned the kiss with fire and teasing of her own, a dart of tongue, a nibble on his lower lip, a tempting molding of her body against his.

He picked her up and carried her to the bed. The old mattress sagged under their double weight, cupping them together in seductive intimacy. He pushed her robe and his shirt aside until there was nothing between her breasts and his chest. He moved the upper half of his body over hers, his mat of silky chest hair tantalizing against her nipples. Her healthy passions responded to the touch and the smoky desire in his eyes, and his sweet tenderness wound itself around her heart. Her fingernails scraped his back lightly, deeper than a caress, not deep enough to scratch. She explored the texture of soft male earlobe and hard cords of throat as his head moved down to her breasts and sent her senses into dizzy spins.

But Miss Prudence, ever cautious and wary of being swept away on a magic carpet of desire and swirling senses, suddenly kicked reckless Tanya back into her closet. Lynn curled her fingers into her palms to make closed fists that couldn't make dangerous forays into male territory. She wedged her arms between them to stop the sweet assault.

Mike instantly sensed the change and responded to it with sensitive tenderness. He twisted a wisp of her hair between his fingers and tickled her cheek with it.

"Second thoughts?" he asked softly.

"What makes you think there were any *first* thoughts?"

He laughed with sweet, knowing intimacy. There had been first thoughts. They both knew it.

He voiced what had been wordless between them. "Stay with me tonight," he whispered. "You know all my deep, dark secrets now. I have nothing left to hide ... and everything to share."

"A brave man, or perhaps a foolish one, considering what happened the last time you made that invitation," she murmured. She turned his hand to tickle his own jaw with the strand of her hair.

"Perhaps a man falling in love *is* both brave and foolish," he suggested.

The soft words made her breath catch and sent odd little tendrils curling to some deep inner place where emotions and senses blended. Yet he hadn't said he was falling in love, only that it was a possibility.

"Perhaps a woman would also have to be brave and foolish to fall in love with a four-personality man," she said.

"But she'd never be bored," he pointed out. "There'd be Tristan to sweep her off her feet and make love to her with the burning intensity of arrogant passion—" He kissed her again, one hand reaching under her to cup her body boldly against the hardness of his, aggressive and conquering.

"She'd have Barry, who, though staid and a bit dull, likes to be very thorough about everything." His kisses went to her neck, to the soft hollow at the base of her throat, to the rounded slopes of her breasts, leaving no inch untouched. He was so thorough in rousing her desire that when he reached the sensitive nipples her body moved restlessly with yearning.

"Plus Mike, of course, who thinks making love should be fun and playful as well as passionate." His tongue moved down to tickle her navel. "Mike wants to make love to you on the hearthstone in the laird's chamber and on that enormous table in the dining room. He wants to have pillow fights and make love to you among a million flying feathers, splash in the bathtub with you and write 'kiss here' in bubbles all over your body."

"And the bumbling old baron?"

"The old baron may bumble, but he has staying power. He'll always be in love with the same woman." He kissed her again, a Rolls-Royce of a kiss, warmer than any heated swimming pool, more precious than any antique.

Lynn laughed softly at the images he created. "The woman who falls in love with a four-personality man would have an entire male harem of lovers, a different one for every mood." Tanya the Temptress was creeping out again, slyly moving her body seductively against his, sending fingertips exploring. Her mind spun in dreamy slow motion, drifting among a delicious smorgasbord of MacNorris men.

"Exactly. And right now—"

The springs creaked as he lifted his body and reached for the button on his jeans, but the small noise sent an echo of alarm to her spinning mind.

She put her hands between them again, suddenly remembering something. "What about Melody? She thinks she's in love with you and probably that you're in love with her, too."

"Melody is sweet and bubbly and vulnerable. Tristan should have his behind kicked for taking advantage of that." Mike scowled slightly as he braced his body over hers with his elbows.

"What do you mean?"

"I told you Tristan wasn't above playing one woman off against another. He is not your all-around nice guy."

"You can't get by with blaming this on Tristan," Lynn warned. "*You* are Tristan."

He nodded in regretful agreement. "I was attracted to you the minute I saw you," he said. "But I was angry, too, at the way I thought you'd tricked me. And so, out of a certain foolish spite, Tristan ignored you and gave all his attention to Melody, doing it so high-handedly, of course, that you'd be sure to *know* you were being ignored. Although it was really you he was interested in all the time. Didn't I warn you this was all very complicated?"

"Especially for Melody," Lynn murmured. "What is 'Tristan'—" she deliberately put the name in vocal quotation marks "—going to do about that?"

"Tristan is going to tell her to go back to Lance in the States, because Lance is the guy she really loves. Melody, too, is afraid of commitment. Always has been, since her father walked out. She loved him very much and it devastated her when he simply abandoned the family. Deep down she was afraid if she loved that much again, the man would also disappear."

"I never knew all that." Lynn drew her head back against the down comforter to look up at him wonderingly. Two years she had roomed with Melody without hearing a word of that, but Tristan—Mike—had found it out in only a few conversations. She considered him with new respect.

"But I can tell from what she says about him that Lance isn't going to disappear on her," Mike added. "He loves her. And Tristan is going to convince her of that. Okay?"

Lynn nodded, hoping it would work the way Mike intended. "Just one more question. Why did you give the baron laryngitis?" She felt like the heroine in some Gothic mystery; they were on the last page, wrapping up all the loose ends.

"Because I knew I couldn't carry off a talking role as an old Scottish baron for an entire evening. I said I was an actor. I didn't say I was a very *good* actor," he reminded. "Those few minutes on the phone with you that first time stretched my capabilities as a full-blooded old Scottish baron to the limits."

"Perhaps you're a better actor than you give yourself credit for," she suggested. "Your acting ability had me and everyone else convinced you were four separate people."

Even now, with him in her arms, images of his separate, in-the-flesh personalities kept flitting through her mind. What he had done suddenly seemed wildly improbable. There were clues: Tristan's inexpert accent; the contrast between his blond hair and dark-haired legs; the obvious similarities in height and build and voice among the MacNorris men; the identical moles; the peculiar way the men were never seen together.

Yet who would instantly put all that together and deduce the unlikely fact that there were not four MacNorris males, but only one? Not Lynn, obviously.

"And now I have a couple of questions for you," he said. "We've covered my sins rather thoroughly, but just *why* did I find you hiding in my closet?"

"I decided I couldn't lay all the castle problems on that sweet, bumbling old baron, which I suspect is what you were counting on." She lifted questioning eyebrows and he nodded guiltily. "So I came over here to jump on Barry about the problems. When he wasn't here I started going through the papers on the desk. I didn't want to be caught doing that, of course, and one thing led to another, which led to your closet. Angry?''

He had shifted his weight to one side as they talked, and he traced sensuous figure-eights around her breast. He grinned and centered each loop with a teasing flick of his tongue. "Not particularly. And I'm sure that, having looked at the papers, you know I'm not making up anything about all the financial problems."

True. "And your other question?" she asked.

He seemed to have forgotten there was another question. His eyes were half closed as his hand stroked the length of her body, the sensations he roused much more than skin deep. They were some distance away from the heater, but Lynn's body had an internal heat flowing. But she could also feel conflicts simmering within her, clashes between head and heart, skirmishes between wary thoughts and eager senses.

At that moment Castle Cat, ever curious, chose to jump on the bed and investigate what was going on. Mike pushed him away with a sweep of one hand. "Hey, cat, get out of here. This is my territory."

Territory apparently reminded him of his other question. He braced himself on one elbow, one hand centered possessively on her abdomen. "How come you were fooling around with all three of these guys anyway?" he asked with mild indignation.

"They were all you," she pointed out.

"*I* knew I was just one guy all the time, but *you* didn't know it."

Lynn had to admit that she, too, after such a long dry spell in her feelings toward men, had been puzzled by this sudden unlikely attraction to three different men.

"Perhaps you're simply irresistible in any form," she suggested. She teased him with a figure-eight pattern of her own, slim fingers combing sensuously through his curly, silky chest hair.

"But what if I really were three different guys?" he persisted. He caught her hand. "Fingers, be good," he commanded, as if they were some separate entity. "How can a man trust a woman who is so fickle?"

"Because, with three different, irresistible guys all rolled into one, how could a woman possibly have time or inclination to look elsewhere?" she answered with teasing logic. And to herself she added, *one confusing, bewildering, mysterious, exciting patchwork of a man!* Trying to follow him through all this was like being caught in a passing whirlwind.

"They all feel the same about you, you know," he whispered. His gaze touched her eyes and throat and lingered on her mouth. He caressed her cheek lightly with his fingertips.

"And how is that?"

"Need you really ask?" The desire was in the smoky depths of his eyes and the pressure of his body.

Her breath caught as his fingertips wandered to her lips and outlined them with a sensuous roughness. She tried to summon the cautious, sensible part of her, but Mike's foot slid up and down the calf of her leg and a tingle followed each stroke. The tingles washed gently up her leg and into her body. They drifted through her mind in lazy waves, blurring any lingering remnants of caution.

He kissed her lips and breasts and body, and her hands wandered over the taut muscles of his back. She was out of the robe by then, no part of her held back from the searing touch of his lips and hands. And this time, when he started to shed the remainder of his clothing, she didn't try to stop him.

Yet stop he did, as abruptly as if a switch had shut off. Lynn's eyes flew open in alarm.

Mike's body was rigid, expression pained and astonished. A yellow-orange, whiskered cat face peered over his shoulder.

Lynn struggled to sit up. "What's wrong?"

"I have been attacked by a cat. In the middle of the most important love scene of my life, I have been pounced on by a *cat*." He sounded as disbelieving as he had when he first realized Lynn had poured cold coffee down his pajamas.

Castle Cat jumped off Mike's back and sat on the edge of the bed, innocently washing one paw.

Lynn didn't want to laugh. She was well aware of the fragility of the male ego in certain situations, but Castle Cat had such a smug expression on his face, as if he were quite aware of what he'd interrupted. Jealous, that's what he'd been, jealous because no one had been paying attention to him. And he'd had his revenge.

"Okay, cat, you've had it," Mike said grimly. "You're going *out*."

Lynn touched his arm. "It really won't make any difference," she said softly. She felt as if she'd just emerged from some steamy room of swirling fog, except that this hot fog had been within her. And now she was back in open air, mind clearing.

He eased his body back over hers. "What do you mean?"

"I'm really not a one-night-stand sort of person." She said it a little helplessly, halfway wishing she were that kind of person, but the minor, sometimes rebellious parts of her personality couldn't change what the larger part of her really was. "I'm just . . . not."

"It wouldn't be just one night. There's tomorrow night and the next and afternoons in between. . . ."

"You know what I mean," she said.

He nodded. "I suppose I do." He sounded more resigned than angry.

She started to squirm out from under him. "My clothes must be dry by now, so I'll just get dressed and—"

He held her with his weight and a leg wound tightly around hers. "No. I want you to stay."

"But—"

"Just stay." He smiled and traced the line of her eyebrows. "In case you haven't noticed, there isn't all that much night left anyway. Listen," he added, tilting his head toward the ceiling.

She listened. Rain was falling again, and here in the cottage it made a cozy, companionable patter that was missing in the castle. They moved under the covers, but Lynn was between the sheets and Mike on top of them.

"Just in case untrustworthy Tristan gets ideas," he said.

"Tristan is the only one with ideas?"

"I'm afraid we're a trio of rogues," he admitted.

"I'm not too sure that old baron is to be trusted, either," Lynn suggested.

"You could be right."

But then, she also wasn't certain *she* was all that trustworthy, and she attempted to keep the sheet as at least a symbolic barrier between them. Although it did have a treacherous tendency to slip down as skin sought skin.

Lynn told Mike about her own multiple personalities. Miss Prudence, who plodded away at the job at SunnyDay, intent on security. Nice Nancy, conventional as a suburban housewife. And, a little reluctantly, she told about Tanya the Temptress, as well.

"Tanya wants to do wild and passionate things," she said with a certain disapproval. "Take chances. Dance naked in the moonlight. Drive men wild with desire."

Mike laughed softly. "Would she settle for driving just one man wild with desire? Because she's already done it, you know."

They talked of other things, too, watched over by a furry yellow-orange chaperon. They listened to the rain and laughed about her suspicions that Barry was surreptitiously stripping the castle of its treasures for his personal gain and that there was some conspiracy against the baron among the younger MacNorris men. They talked of what Mike hoped to do with the castle. He had another group of guests scheduled to arrive three days after Lynn's group left.

"And do you know how many guests will there be?" she inquired.

"It's the first question I ask these days."

"Then all this hasn't been for nothing," she said.

"It wouldn't have been for nothing even if I hadn't learned that lesson," he said meaningfully. "Because I found *my* private harem in you."

But it was a temporary find, she thought bleakly. Because he was a baron in Scotland and she was a secretary in California, and at the end of the week their lives would separate like some inevitable earthquake movement along the San Andreas Fault.

He massaged the remaining soreness out of her back, and she worried slightly that Melody might be concerned about her absence during the night and send out a search party. However, given Melody's habit of falling into a serene slumber the minute she got into bed, it wasn't a large worry.

In the early morning Mike slipped over to the castle and returned with breakfast for two—juice and coffee, sausage and eggs, toast and jam and the broiled half-tomato that Lynn had rather come to like.

"Was the cook curious about why you wanted such a large breakfast?" she asked as they ate.

"The cook was in too foul a mood to notice what I was doing. It seems someone crept into her kitchen domain during the night and made fudge. At least fudge is what it looked like, from the mess of chocolate-covered pans and counter."

"I'm sorry," Lynn said a little helplessly. She went on to explain how the group had been assembled and how little she knew most of the people. "I had no idea they'd behave like this."

"But the idea of getting twenty people together was yours."

She nodded agreement. "I'm afraid so."

After breakfast Mike took Lynn down the hall to show her another room in the cottage. It held an intriguing assortment of strange items. The decapitated helmet of a suit of armor. A stuffed deer, slightly moth-eaten. Bits of broken furniture. Tattered clothes of a long-gone period. A broken lance. A lamp with a cracked chimney.

"What is all this?" she asked. She fingered a somewhat quizzical-looking stuffed bird.

"The castle junk heap, I guess. It was all like this when I came."

"What a marvelous place to play on a rainy day!" she exclaimed, moving around to touch a plumed hat and a pair of mismatched shoes.

"It's raining now. What would you like to play?"

She put the helmet from the suit of armor on him, and draped a bit of tartan over his shoulder. She held a worn velvet gown to her chest and began with a melodramatic, "Sir, I beseech thee—"

But just at that moment the bell jangled, signifying that someone was at the cottage door.

Mike looked in the direction of the office as if he were inclined to ignore the bell. But conscientious Barry won out. He removed the armored helmet. "Duty calls," he said regretfully.

"And I've got to get back to the castle."

"You'll come back to play another time?" He touched her cheek softly.

"We'll see."

He looked as if he were inclined to argue the vagueness of that answer, but by then the doorbell sounded like a fire alarm.

"Tell Melody that Tristan wants to see her, okay? Nine o'clock. I'll pick her up in the car."

Lynn nodded. Mike went to the front office, and Lynn tiptoed into the bedroom. She dressed quickly. Her clothes looked a bit worse for wear after their dip in the bathtub, but perhaps she could sneak up to her room without anyone noticing. She slipped out the back way, echoes of the cook's angry voice reaching all the way to the rear door.

Melody wasn't in the room when Lynn got there. Lynn had changed clothes by the time Melody returned from breakfast.

"What did you do, get up and take an early walk?" Melody asked, apparently unaware of Lynn's night-long absence.

Lynn made a noncommittal murmur that might have been yes or no. "Oh, by the way, I ran into Tristan. He wants to see you. He'll pick you up in the car at nine o'clock."

"Why don't you find your Mike, and we'll all sneak off together for the day? We could have a marvelous time!"

"No, I...uh...think Mike will be busy," Lynn said with an inner smile at the secret she knew.

Melody dashed out alone when the car and chauffeur pulled up in front of the castle to the grumblings of others suggesting that certain people were monopolizing the facilities. Lynn brightly suggested the rest of the group drive to Loch Lomond for the day.

It was not a memorably successful idea. They arrived too late to go on the boat tour of the loch. At Lynn's urging they all tried the Scottish dish haggis for lunch, hated it and blamed her. The rain came down so heavily that they finally gave up and returned to the castle at midafternoon.

Lynn was uncertain what to expect from Melody, but she was beaming happily. She said Tristan had given her marvelous advice, she'd already called Lance and she was going to go home and marry him.

Lynn hugged her. "It's really what you wanted all along, isn't it?"

Melody nodded. "It just took Tristan to make me see it. He really is a terrific guy, you know. The only thing I'm sorry about is that now you'll have to find a new roommate."

"I'm sorry about that too, but mostly I'm just happy for you." They hugged again.

"Oh, Tristan said Barry would like to see you in his office when you got back."

That surprised Lynn, but she hurried over to the cottage immediately. She rang the bell, and then stepped inside without waiting for an answer. "Mike? You here?"

"I'm in here changing."

"Clothes?"

"Personalities."

"You must have done a great job with Melody," Lynn called to him. She reported on the results of the conversation.

The phone rang while she was talking to him, and he came out to answer it. The caller was obviously some irate creditor who hadn't been paid. Even as she regretted all his financial problems, Lynn smiled as she watched Mike on the phone. His metamorphosis was not quite complete. He'd removed the blond wig but not the mustache. He was still wearing Tristan's kilt, but with it was Barry's conservative-businessman jacket and tie.

"We have another problem now," he said when he put the phone down. Lynn noted that in his distraction he had used the term we, as if it were her problem, too.

"The person on the phone?"

He dismissed the phone call with a gesture of one hand. "He merely wants my money or my life. Nothing vital."

"Melody said you wanted to see me. Nothing too serious, I hope. The natives are restless." She nodded toward the castle. "I talked them into haggis for lunch and they're ready to cast me into the dungeon. I hope the cook has something tasty planned for supper to soothe them."

"I don't think so," Mike said. "That's the latest problem. The cook quit."

Chapter Nine

Because of the fudge disaster?'' Lynn asked.

"That was the breaking point. Although she's been unhappy all along that I've never hired the kitchen assistant she was supposed to have to do the dishes. And I can't blame her for being angry about that. There have been a *lot* of dishes."

"Because of my arrival with a cast of thousands." Lynn sighed. She put her arms around him from behind, cheek against his back. "Can I do something to help?"

"How good a cook are you?"

Lynn made a regretful murmur. She could manage reasonably well for one or two people. She could even do an occasional dinner party for eight or ten. But two meals a day for twenty people? No. Not if they expected anything more than cornflakes for breakfast and hot dogs for dinner.

They both jumped as the doorbell rang. Mike retreated a step toward the hallway, but it was too late; Melody had already opened the door and peeked inside.

Her lips parted and her eyes widened in bewilderment. She glanced back and forth between them, her gaze finally stopping on Mike, caught like some exotic hybrid between his Barry and Tristan personalities. Lynn realized her hand still lingered with incriminating intimacy on his waist.

Instead of removing it, she looked at Mike and said, "I think we should tell Melody. She can keep a secret."

"Yes," Melody agreed. "Somebody tell me something."

Mike explained, condensing the story from what he'd told Lynn, but bringing it up to the current moment. Lynn added a bit about her own multiple personalities, hoping that would make what Mike had done sound less wildly incredible. She was afraid that Melody might be angry at her and accuse her of latching on to Tristan for herself, but after the first moments of shock, Melody's usual good humor bubbled through.

She started laughing, and then Mike told about the complicated problems of trying to be four men . . . sometimes forgetting which one he was, getting an excruciatingly itchy place under his mustache, feeling his wig lifting precariously in a breeze. He did a wicked imitation of the cook telling him he was "daft as a doited clown," and then they were all laughing, holding on to the desk and each other for support as the laughter made their eyes water and knees wobble.

They all felt better when the laughter finally died away, but nothing was solved, of course. Mike said he'd try to locate another cook, but he doubted he'd be able to find someone before the week ended.

"I'd just refund everyone's money and tell them to go home, but I've spent part of it, of course," he added unhappily. "How violent will they become when they find there are no meals?"

It was a question Lynn did not like to contemplate, but Melody put a forefinger to her chin in the way she did when she was thinking hard. "I think you're underestimating them," she said finally.

"Who?" Lynn asked. Her mind was still on cooks.

"Them. Us. The Group, as you put it."

"Melody, hon, you weren't there today when the Haggis Rebellion broke out! They are in a very nasty mood, and I doubt that a dose of truth will put them in a better one."

"I think you're wrong," Melody said in one of her rare shows of stubbornness. "Both of you have been telling me about your multiple personalities, and I think all of us do have them, to some degree at least. I know I do. And I think if you tell the other guests about this predicament that the better, nicer part of their personalities will come out and be understanding."

Mike looked doubtful, but he finally nodded, although with more resignation than confidence. "I guess it's worth a try."

He told them to assemble the other guests, and he'd come over and talk to them in about an hour.

Lynn and Melody got the other guests together, although not without considerable grumbling, and not without growing apprehension on Lynn's part. The Group, she suspected, had turned into The Hungry Mob after their dissatisfaction with lunch. She had visions of boos and hisses at best, outright lynching at worst when they learned of the current meal situation.

She assumed Mike would arrive looking like Mike, but it was the baron who entered the room, silvery-haired and elegant. There was a little flurry of excitement. The baron raised one hand for quiet. He had a bulging sack in the other hand.

"Aye, and it's a sorry tale I have to tell ye," he began in a melancholy tone, with a downward stroke of silver mustache. "I dinna know where to start."

But he did start, his gruff Scottish burr gradually changing to an American sound that was more understandable to his audience as he told of inheriting the castle and the ensuing financial problems. His back also gradually straightened, going from an old man's bent curve to a younger man's straightness, as if he were shedding years as he spoke. Which, in a way, he was, although he made the changes so subtly that Lynn wasn't certain anyone but she was consciously aware of them.

"And then I chose a solution that some of you may think devious and others find bizarre. You see, I needed more people around the castle to serve you, and I hadn't the money to hire them, so I chose an...ah...unusual way to spread myself around. I truly am Baron Conor MacNorris, but I'm afraid I have deceived you a bit even on that matter."

He stripped off the mustache first, which made his audience straighten up and take notice. Surprised gasps followed the removal of his face makeup and wig.

"You see, under all this I am—" he took off the tartan plaid jacket, replaced it with a dark business-suit jacket from the sack, and added heavy-rimmed glasses "—Barry MacNorris, the secretary handling business affairs here."

"Well, I'll be darned," Reva said, which seemed to express the general view of amazement.

"But I'm afraid that wasn't my only deception." From the sack came another wig and mustache. The mustache was a bit lopsided above his upper lip when he applied it, but Tristan was definitely there before them. He took the kilt out of the sack and held it up to his waist, using Tristan's macho swagger to stride this way and that and model it for them.

"And that isn't all."

One more presto-change, and he became Mike, the handyman-gardener. Tousled hair, boyish grin, rough workshirt.

Stunned silence followed. Lynn held her breath.

And then Kristie suddenly started applauding. "That's marvelous! I love it!"

After a moment's hesitation the others seemed to come out of their shock and joined in.

Reva went up and pumped his hand. "You were terrific. I never suspected."

Relief flooded through Lynn as everyone crowded around to ask questions, but it was a short-lived relief. Okay, so they weren't going to tear him apart like a pack of angry wolves. They hadn't heard all of it yet, and when they learned there was no longer a cook to prepare meals, they just might turn into snarling wolves. She still wasn't as confident as Melody was that inside each of them lurked someone decent and understanding.

Mike started out by explaining the details of what had become of the Rolls-Royce, why there were no trout in the trout ponds, no heat in the heated pool, no coal for the fireplaces. Another stunned silence followed his final announcement that now there was also no cook.

"About all I can do is tell you how sorry I am you've had such a miserable vacation, refund what's left of your money and give you my promise that I'll return the balance as soon as I can. I hope you won't have any problems changing dates for your return flights home."

Lynn expected an immediate mass exodus of people rushing upstairs to pack and leave, but to her surprise everyone just sat there looking more bemused than anxious to catch a flight home.

Finally Lily Dunbar rose from the sofa she had occupied ever since she'd decided she was on her deathbed. She threw away her blanket as if she were discarding a death shroud. "I am a marvelous cook," she announced with no pretense of humility. "My sit-down dinners for thirty are practically legendary." She swept toward the kitchen as if she had a tiara on her head and a ten-foot train following.

"Well, I can certainly do waitress or maid work," Reva said, obviously not wanting to be outdone.

A couple of the men volunteered to get firewood, if there were any more trees that could be cut up. Chris and Christy, after exchanging guilty looks that told Lynn they were probably the fudge bandits, said they could handle kitchen cleanup and dishes.

"Look, this all sounds great," Mike said, "and I thank you for your understanding. But I can't expect you to spend your vacations doing castle chores."

Bill Myerson, the accountant, stepped forward. "I'm willing to let you keep all I've paid for the week. No refund. Plus, since I'm not much on household chores, I'll offer some professional advice on financial management. I'll look on it as kind of a working vacation."

"That sounds good," Mike agreed cautiously. He looked pleasantly surprised, but wary, as if he expected something more was coming. It was.

With an accountant's shrewdness Bill Myerson added, "But it's not an entirely altruistic gesture on my part, because there's a provision that in exchange I get a week next year without charge. And perhaps some of the other guests would like a similar deal."

Lynn saw Mike swallow. It was a fairly hard bargain. A full week with all the usual expenses for food and castle upkeep, and no income. But it offered Mike a chance to keep going *now*, to prepare for the next group of guests. After a long hesitation he nodded.

"Anyone else want the same deal?" Bill asked.

In the end, all but three people did, Melody among them, because she'd be married by then. She was, in fact, leaving the following day, anxious now to get back to Lance.

"There's no point not enjoying ourselves while we're here," said one of the guys who was involved in the legal dispute over the dissolution of the partnership business. "I was looking at the heating system out at the pool, and I think I might be able to do something with it."

"I could probably help," said his former partner with elaborate nonchalance.

"Do either of you know anything about this sort of thing?" Lynn asked doubtfully.

"We had a repair business together," the first man said.

"It was . . . ah . . . personality conflicts, not lack of expertise, that did in our partnership," the other said.

Lynn thought that comment might bring on a new skirmish, but the two men merely looked at each other warily. One started out the door toward the pool and after a moment's hesitation the other followed. Lynn doubted if it was peace between them, but apparently there was a temporary truce.

The Group organized itself with astonishing efficiency. They made up teams of maids, waitresses, housecleaners, dishwashers, woodcutters, yardmen.

"I guess the MacNorris magic worked," Lynn said after everyone had scattered to their tasks. She felt a little dazed, as if she'd just been caught in a small stampede.

"No. Melody was right. Most people really do have a pretty decent side buried in there somewhere. That along with the good old American way of rallying round and pulling together when the going gets tough."

"Now if someone could just figure out how to get the Rolls-Royce back," Lynn teased. Mike just rolled his eyes.

Lily served a succulent beef roast with a marvelous sauce for dinner, tender-crisp vegetables, salad with a dressing made from a recipe that she claimed a famous French chef had given her as a token of their friendship, and an airy meringue thing for dessert. Mike ate with them. Lynn and Melody kept the waitress jobs that they were by now familiar with. After the meal Mike and several men took the truck out to haul in firewood. Later they built a roaring blaze in the fireplace, and Mike entertained them with a scene from one of his far, far, off-Broadway plays. It had probably been dramatic and serious at one time, but with Mike energetically playing all the parts with outrageous melodrama, it was pure comic mayhem.

Afterward, Reva said she'd make coffee, but Lily, who had turned into more of a kitchen tyrant than the original Scottish cook had ever thought of being, haughtily said she would take care of it. Her health now appeared to be excellent.

Mike excused himself a little later, but his eyes signaled that he wanted Lynn to meet him outside. She hesitated about doing so. She knew what he wanted. And she was feeling all soft and warm and happy about the way things had turned out, proud of him, and terribly vulnerable to his charm. She knew she was in a much too susceptible mood to risk much more exposure to him tonight.

But go she did, of course. The rain had stopped and the moon silvered the old castle with a timeless magic. Mike was waiting for her just outside the cottage, Castle Cat purring at his feet.

"Congratulations," she said. "Everyone is having a terrific time now."

He put his arms around her and kissed her on the nose. "I know how the two of us could have an even more terrific time," he said meaningfully.

"For a man with four personalities, you have an awfully one-track mind," she chided.

"Okay, let's take a walk then. I want to talk to you about something."

A walk seemed safer than various other possibilities. He put his left arm around her shoulders, and she slipped her right arm around his waist. They strolled toward the troutless trout ponds, dark water crossed by a silvery moonpath. Castle Cat walked with them, apparently assuming that "three's a crowd" didn't apply if one of the three was a cat.

"What did you want to talk to me about?" Lynn asked.

"You like it here, don't you?"

Lynn nodded. "I haven't even begun to see and do everything I'd like to in Scotland."

"But you didn't commit yourself on the return week next year."

So he'd noticed that.

He stopped and turned her to face him. "Lynn, I don't want to lose you," he said with a husky catch in his voice.

The moonlight sculpted his face with aristocratic hollows and planes.

"I don't want to lose you, either," she said honestly. She paraphrased an old saying. "But Scotland is Scotland, and California is California, and never the twain shall meet. Maybe you'll get over to the States sometime?"

He shook his head. "Not for a long time anyway. I have my work cut out for me here. But you could be with me—"

She looked up at him, startled. But before her heart had time for more than a few explosive thuds, he explained the statement.

"You're not really happy with your job at the greeting-card company back in the States. It's dull and boring—"

"Secure and dependable," she corrected. "With excellent fringe benefits."

His hands lightly massaging her shoulders dismissed security and fringe benefits as irrelevant.

"You could stay here, be *my* secretary—"

She laughed lightly. "And what other roles would I be playing? Upstairs maid? Castle guide?" *Part-time lover?* "Do you supply wigs, or must I provide my own?"

"No, really. I'm offering you an honest-to-gosh secretarial job. If I had a competent secretary, it would free me to do a lot of other things that aren't getting done, and I wouldn't miss phone calls from prospective guests. I couldn't pay as much as you've been making back home, but there'd be room and board and a very congenial boss—" He proved that with a teasing kiss on the corner of her mouth.

"A boss who would pay me with hugs and kisses and IOUs?"

He sighed. "Not secure enough, huh?"

"The castle may be repossessed by some dastardly villain at any moment, and then where would I be?"

"You'd still have me."

But that wouldn't necessarily be true, whether or not a dastardly villain grabbed the castle. Because Mike-Tristan shunned commitment. He might abandon her as he had abandoned careers; she had visions of herself, penniless, heartbroken, trying to hitchhike or stow away on a homeward-bound jet.

"You don't have to tell me yes right now, just don't tell me no, okay?" He spoke swiftly, as if to forestall some hasty negative decision on her part. "There's still Thursday and Friday for you to consider it."

The two days loomed up before her like huge, luminous jewels—with the days of her life following afterward merely dull cardboard cutouts.

At the trout pond most distant from the castle, Mike spread his jacket on the damp grass. Lynn hesitated. They should keep walking. She knew what would happen if they sat down. It was inevitable.

Yes, walking was much safer than sitting. She had the shaky feeling that if she ever once made love with him she would be lost, that she would throw all good sense and caution to the winds and find herself adrift on a dangerous sea of love, with nothing to anchor her, willing to do anything, go anywhere for him.

"Oh, look, what's that on the hillside beyond the pond?" Lynn asked brightly. It was a rock-walled area with the dull gleam of something rocky or metallic within. She tugged on his sleeve. "Let's go over and see."

Mike put his arms around her from the back and kissed the side of her throat. "I'd much rather sit here with you in my arms and watch the moonlight," he whispered.

Lynn put her hands on his but didn't try to free herself from the circle of his arms. She made a small sigh of defeat as his lips whispered kisses on her throat and ear and nape, but she raised one more defense. "And talk?"

"You talk," he said. "I'll listen."

They sat on the jacket, his back braced against a tree, her back against his chest. His hands rested lightly, innocently, at her waist. His legs curved warmly around her. Castle Cat, fickle chaperon that he was, dashed off to investigate a rustle in the trees.

Lynn chattered with bright irrelevance about the Loch Lomond boat trip they'd missed, about tasting some marvelous, brown-sugary candy in a gift shop and looking at antique keys with Kristie. But her mind kept losing track of what she intended to say, distracted by the tip of his tongue tracing the curve of her ear and the sides of his thumbs wandering up to caress the underside of her breasts.

And when he sank lower against the tree and turned her to face him, her words drifted off into the small, unidentifiable little rustles and squeaks of the night. Her mouth lifted to meet his, and then she was conscious only of him. His tongue made a sweet, lazy invasion, seductive as some slow-moving dance. She drifted in the dance with him, tongue advancing when his retreated.

She felt her resistance slipping away, or perhaps it was desire rising to engulf it. He unbuttoned her blouse, letting the moonlight flood her breasts. He laughed softly, delightedly, at the wisp of black-net bra covering them. His fingertip traced the outline of a tiny silver butterfly embroidered into the net.

"Cold?" he whispered as a tremor went through her. He didn't wait for an answer. He retrieved the edges of the blouse, but when he drew them together his face was between them, blouse half covering his head like a silken tent. Under cover he ravished her breasts with kisses, gentle tug of lips, tantalizing pressure of teeth. He circled the full roundness with his tongue, spirals climbing again and again to the sensitive peaks.

And when his hand dipped between the taut plane of her belly and the triangle of lace covering it, she groaned softly.

"This isn't fair, Mike," she whispered.

"What isn't fair?"

"Making me want you so much that I start thinking all kinds of wild and crazy things...."

He drew back and smiled. "Like dancing naked in the moonlight? I'll dance with you, you know."

No, it wasn't dancing in the moonlight that his seductive kisses and caresses made her think about. They made her think of recklessly loving him here in the moonlight, of abandoning all that was safe and secure back home and accepting his will-o'-the-wisp offer of a job and the intimate relationship that she knew went with it.

"It isn't fair, Mike," she whispered again.

She thought he was going to ignore her plea, keep up the sensuous assault that was already so close to breaking through her barriers.

But instead what he said was, "Maybe you're right." His tone was odd, not angry, but different, as if he'd peered through some inward window and seen something he hadn't noticed before. "Do you want to walk over there?" He gestured to the walled area on the slope. "It's an old family cemetery."

Lynn buttoned her blouse and stood up. Her clothes, where his jacket hadn't protected them from the ground, held a hint of the earth's dampness. Mike put his jacket on, seeming oblivious to the fact that it was even wetter. They circled the pond and climbed the sloping hillside. The old iron gate squeaked when Mike opened it. Lynn knew she'd have been disappointed if it hadn't, because an old cemetery gate was surely meant to squeak.

They wandered among the gravestones that gleamed softly in the moonlight, inscribed with MacNorris names, names going back to the early seventeen hundreds, others even older, so weathered that neither name nor dates could be discerned. The late baron's gravestone shone new among the older stones, beside it was his wife's stone. But the feeling here among these remnants of lives past was oddly more of peace and serenity than sadness.

"Maybe I'll be buried here, too, someday," Mike said. He was halfsitting, halfleaning against an old rose-gray gravestone, not in disrespect but with a lack of the uneasiness some people feel in such surroundings. He smiled, softening the serious comment by adding, "Unless your 'dastardly villain' takes over the place. And if he does, I'm going to return from wherever I'm at and become a castle ghost to haunt him until he'll be happy to return it to some deserving MacNorris."

"With your multipersonality talents, you could probably be *four* ghosts," Lynn teased. "You'll drive the poor folks crazy."

But what he said made her realize more than ever that once she went home, they probably never would see each other again. He might be unwilling or unable to commit himself in a relationship, but he was committed to *here*. They might try to keep a long-distance relationship going for a while, she hoping it might someday lead to commitment, he hoping she'd abandon a need for promises and security. But eventually whatever tenuous relationship they had would fade like the ink on an old love letter.

"I hope you'll think some more about what we were discussing earlier," he said. "I want you here. I want to be with you." He looped his arms around her and pulled her into the angle of his spread legs. She was, as always, so aware of the virile maleness of him, the feeling that if she didn't keep control she might make wild, carefree love with him on the spot, even here.

But his words, softly, even lovingly spoken, aroused a contrasting surge of anger and resentment. He could commit himself to a pile of stone—that's all the castle was really, chunks of stone arranged in fairy-tale shape—and a piece of land. But that was *all* he would commit to. And now she was in love with him.

Oh, no, she told herself firmly. Whoa there, Tanya and anyone else in there with such rash ideas. We may be a bit infatuated, but *love*? Let's not exaggerate.

"I'd better be getting back to the castle," Lynn said. "I have to be up early to set the table for breakfast."

They walked back holding hands, but there was a certain stiffness between them. Castle Cat came out to meet them as they approached the castle, his meow querulous. Lynn thought Mike might come up with another suggestion that she spend the night with him. In fact, she was reasonably certain he was going to do it when they got to the door at the rear of the castle.

He held both her hands and looked down at her for a long minute. She couldn't see his eyes, but she knew they were that smoky blue of MacNorris desire. But he simply kissed her lightly on the mouth and walked away.

Her lips parted and she almost called him back. So little time left, and they were going to spend it apart instead of together. Why hadn't he asked her to stay with him tonight? Okay, so she'd rejected similar invitations two or three times already. Why hadn't the Tristan part of him boldly rejected *her* rejections? Mike wasn't a man to let rejection daunt him, and Tristan was fully capable of arrogantly sweeping her up in his arms and carrying her off to his bed.

Not that the reason mattered, she thought dispiritedly as she climbed the circular stairway. In fact, it was undoubtedly better this way. Perhaps a two-day drawing apart would soften the blow of the final separation.

Lily Dunbar prepared a marvelous breakfast and announced that, if it was all right with Mike, she would also serve a lunch. After clearing the breakfast dishes for Chris and Christy to wash, Lynn joined the housecleaning team. They dusted and scrubbed, took turns running an ancient vacuum cleaner over carpets, even did the interior of a few windows. The men brought wood for the fireplaces, and Lynn caught occasional glimpses of others whipping the grounds into shape. The two repairmen-partners did not appear at lunch. They had driven into Glasgow to see if they could find substitute parts for the swimming-pool heating system. Melody had ridden in with them to catch her plane.

In the afternoon, more cleaning. Lynn suspected it would take a small army of workers a month to *really* clean the castle, but they concentrated on places most visible to guests.

At dinner that evening, Mike had a couple of announcements to make. One was that the swimming-pool heater was now working. It would take some time to circulate and warm all the water, but by morning there should be a noticeable difference in water temperature. The other announcement was that two more castle reservations had been received, and August, the favorite month for holidays in Scotland, was now filled up.

After dinner, Mike gave them a special tour through a secret passageway. Much to Lynn's surprise the tour started in her bedroom, where he pushed aside a wall panel to reveal a cramped corridor. It smelled faintly of dust and disuse, as if the air had been buried there for centuries, although, he, obviously, had been in there before. The corridor wound down and around corners, up, down and around more corners, a flashlight beam sending suitably spooky shadows ahead of them. Nervous giggles trailed behind. Finally the passageway came to a dead end at a bare wall.

"I still haven't figured out where this dead-end point is," Mike said. He ran his fingers all around the edges of the wall, looking for some button or device that would open it, but there was nothing. He tapped his knuckles on the blank wall and got an eerie, hollow sound. "I think it's been boarded up from the other side."

After everyone was out of the passageway, there was speculation, both risqué and spooky, about its past purposes. Through both tour and discussion, Mike treated Lynn no differently than he did any other guest, nor did his eyes signal for some private meeting afterward.

After a late-night snack, everyone drifted off to bed. Lynn's room felt empty without Melody's familiar presence. There was too much space and silence in which to think about Mike and going home.

The gamekeeper's cottage was not visible from Lynn's bedroom window, but on an after-midnight trip to the bathroom she detoured to peer out the long, narrow windows by the curved stairway. From there she could see the peaked-roof silhouette of the cottage. No lights. Mike was probably sleeping sweetly, untroubled by the restless churnings of love that were keeping her sleepless, she thought unhappily. Although it was *possible* that he was lying there awake, desperately wishing she'd come to him.

She mulled that thought in her mind, examining it like some wickedly enticing tidbit dangling before her. She could tiptoe out to the cottage, slip silently through the door, creep up to his bed. Her heart hammered with the delicious appeal of it.

Then something caught her eye. It was movement out at the pool, which was more visible now that the shrubs and bushes had been trimmed. She cupped her hands around her face, nose pressed to the glass as she tried to get a better look. Someone was out there, diving into the pool, swimming back to the edge and diving again. He wasn't wearing swim trunks; it looked as if he had on jeans and long-sleeved shirt.

It was Mike, no doubt about it. She stared, perplexed. Why in the world was he out there at this hour, swimming in such odd attire? The pool may have warmed slightly by now, but it must still be icy cold. Mike, taking a midnight swim, fully dressed, in frigid waters. What a weird and crazy thing to do.

And exactly the sort of strange thing Mike *would* do, she thought with a flutter of excitement and glee. Exactly the sort of thing Tanya the Temptress would do, too!

She started to turn away from the window, usual caution overcome by a midnight recklessness. She'd join him in the pool, sneak up and dive in when he wasn't looking. Yes, she'd do it! He'd give a whoop of joyful laughter. They'd half freeze their silly "arses" off, as the baron would say, and then go back to the cottage arm in arm. They'd dry their clothes in front of the heater and make the most of what time they had together, and maybe, just maybe— Then she saw something else. It was a female figure dashing from the castle across the cut grass to the pool. She couldn't make out who it was, someone dark-haired, gracefully long-legged. Kristie? Reva?

Whoever she was, when she reached the pool she threw off her outer garments and plunged into the pool with Mike. She was wearing either an incredibly skimpy swimming suit . . . or nothing.

And Lynn had thought he was lying alone and lonesome in his cottage, perhaps yearning for her! No way. Her delightful little fantasy screeched to a halt, like a broken bit of videotape.

Mike was neither sleeping nor yearning. Instead he was blithely enjoying an intimate midnight rendezvous with some new and exciting partner and had probably forgotten Lynn even existed.

And he undoubtedly wouldn't be lonesome in his cottage or his bed, afterward, she thought grimly.

Chapter Ten

Lynn inspected The Group carefully as she waited tables at breakfast. There were some late stragglers, but, other than Mike himself, no absentees. She checked for signs of excessive yawning or lethargy that might point to a night of decadent revelry in pool or bedroom. But she sourly decided that with this bunch of amorous gadabouts, that was like searching for one rotten apple among a whole basketful. At least half the guests looked as if they'd been involved in an all-night orgy; the other half looked as if they'd stayed up to watch.

She casually inquired of Lily Dunbar if Mike had taken his breakfast at the cottage and was informed that he had eaten early so he could do some work on the truck.

A group decision was made to spend the morning working and the afternoon swimming and relaxing in preparation for the next day's long flight home. For this, their last day, Scotland turned on all its glorious charm. Blue sky was decorated with friendly puffs of cloud, golden sunshine and fresh-washed air. Yesterday's raindrops were today's jewels, gleaming in spiderwebs and trembling on the edges of leaves. The swans floated with serene elegance on their favorite pond.

Everyone was in a cheerful, playful mood. Everyone but Lynn. She halfway wished the rain had continued. It would have better suited her gloomy mood; a full-fledged hurricane would have suited her mood, in fact.

She resolutely did not let her gloominess show, however. When everyone gathered around the warm pool after lunch, she made a Miss American effort to out-cheerful and out-congeniality everyone. She bubbled relentlessly and flirted outrageously.

Her deception glowed with success. After she had been tossed in the pool for the third time by a trio of male admirers, Mike approached. He had an uncharacteristically surly expression.

"You seem to be enjoying yourself." He made it sound as if she were stealing the castle silverware.

"That's the point of taking a vacation, isn't it?"

"I suppose you're glad to be going home? Back to your fascinating job?"

She ignored the cheap-shot sarcasm. "Vacations are marvelous, but it's always good to get home." That was a favorite expression of her mother's, a virtuous cliché that Lynn had never particularly subscribed to, but which seemed useful at the moment.

He changed the subject. "I had a phone call from the States late last night."

"I hope it didn't interrupt anything—" she fished delicately for a word "—strategic."

He gave her a what-the-hell-is-*that*-supposed-to-mean scowl, to which she just smiled blandly. She still hadn't figured out who'd been playing water nymphet with him the previous night.

"I think I mentioned to you earlier that I'd had some dealings with a company that was interested in the computer games I'd created. They're going to use one of them, and they'll take another after I make a few alterations in it. The money is quite generous, with a potential for considerably more. I'll buy a computer and do the work on the second game next winter during the slack season."

"That's great. I'm very happy for you." It was true. She knew this was something he truly enjoyed. But what he said further emphasized something else she knew, that he had no plans for a flamboyant dash across international waters in romantic pursuit of her. "You'll no longer be an impoverished baron."

"I wouldn't go so far as to say that. It will relieve some of the symptoms of, although not necessarily cure, my financial ailments here. I should be able to guarantee employees something more than IOUs."

She noticed that he did not mention hugs and kisses. "I'm sure that will please your new cook, maid, chauffeur, et cetera."

"I was hoping it would persuade you to reconsider my job offer." He briskly named a specific salary and said she'd have meals and a private room in the castle.

Lynn was surprised at the repeat of the job offer, but she hid it under an evasive question. "Aren't there regulations about foreigners working here?"

"There are formalities of some kind, but nothing insurmountable."

It was all cool and businesslike, not one word that sounded personal, much less intimate. She still refused to classify her feelings for him under the dangerous term "love," but the prospect of watching him indulge in romantic games with some new guest playmate every week did not fill her with joy. Nor did the thought of discovering she *was* hopelessly in love with a man with an openly stated aversion to commitment.

"Well?" Mike prodded.

"I don't think so, Mike. But thanks for the offer." She didn't add elaborate explanations.

"You're trying to force a marriage proposal out of me, aren't you?" Mike demanded with an angry blaze of MacNorris-blue eyes. "Just because I'm—" He broke off whatever he'd started to say and finished with, "Because you're up to your elbows in some neurotic need for commitment and security."

"I'm doing no such thing! And I am *not* neurotic! I'd *never* try to force—" Lynn gasped and sputtered with fury and indignation at the wild accusation. "And I can't think of anything *less* secure than marrying you!"

That ended Lynn's involvement in the pool party. She stormed upstairs to pack, thinking she should have gone home with Melody. She didn't even want to go down for dinner, but she couldn't shirk her waitress responsibilities. Maybe she'd just eat in the kitchen.

She decided against that idea, not wanting to look like some woebegone Cinderella waif while everyone else was partying on Lily's special French dinner and the lavish flow of champagne that Mike had unexpectedly provided. He made a little speech after dinner, thanking everyone for their help and understanding and saying he was looking forward to seeing most of them again next year.

Lynn didn't intend to talk to him, but when she was clearing the table she dropped a plate and Mike strolled over.

"You don't seem to be having as much fun as everyone else," he observed as she scrambled to pick up the broken pieces.

"First you accuse me of having too much fun, now I'm not having enough fun. And the fact of the matter is, how much fun I'm having is none of your concern." She looked at the broken pieces of china in her hands. "I'm sorry I broke the plate. If you'll tell me how much it's worth, I'll pay for it."

He inspected the broken pieces critically. "Seventeen thousand, four hundred ninety-two dollars and seventeen cents. Give or take a dime."

"That's preposterous!"

"If you can't pay for it, you'll have to stay and work it out."

"That's even more preposterous!"

He sighed with theatrical resignation. "Call it a fair exchange, then. Your waitress work for one plate." He handed the broken pieces back to her.

Lynn went up to her room as soon as she could get away. Later, peering out the staircase window, she saw that the party had moved out to the swimming pool. She did not rush out to participate nor to check for swimsuits. She went back to her bedroom, and, for no particular reason she could explain, slid aside the wall panel that concealed the secret passageway. She sat cross-legged and stared gloomily into the shadowy depths.

She'd still have a week of vacation when she got home before she was due back to work at SunnyDay. She could give the apartment a good cleaning. Write letters she owed. Shorten her blue skirt. A week from Monday she'd be back at the office. There wouldn't be much catching up to do. Though Lynn had never been able to understand why, the woman who was filling in for her coveted her job, and was competent and efficient. All Lynn would have to do when she got back to work were the usual dull sales reports, the memos, the charts and the letters, all dutifully ending in "Have yourself a SunnyDay." Then she could file the sales reports, memos, charts and letters.

She made a little paper airplane out of a piece of pink stationery that Melody had left behind. She aimed it into the oblong of the secret passageway. It sailed silently into the darkness and vanished.

Now she knew why she was looking at the secret passageway. That was her future in there. Dark and gloomy. Cramped and dusty. And going nowhere.

In the morning everyone rushed around gathering up belongings and jockeying for bathroom time. Breakfast was early and hurried because their plane left the Glasgow airport at 9:15, but last night's party atmosphere lingered. Lynn resolutely told herself she was glad to be going home, but she kept thinking of all the things she wished she'd done here. Taken more photographs. Met more Scottish people. Visited more historic old castles.

She had packed her large suitcase the night before. She tucked her nightgown and other last-minute items into the cosmetics case. She removed the sheets from her bed and left them in a bundle by the door.

Mike showed up to drive the castle car to the airport as he had met them, in Tristan's kilt, blond wig and mustache. Everyone seemed to look on this as a jolly reminder of a good joke that had been played on them. Lynn, however, suspected that Mike was using the Tristan disguise to send her a deliberate message about the part of him that *was* Tristan. The part that was arrogant, even a little ruthless, the part that scorned commitment.

Lynn purposely rode in one of the other cars. They reached the airport, turned the cars in at the rental agency and checked on their flight. Several times Lynn thought Mike's eyes were on her, but she didn't look at him because she was afraid she'd find it was just wishful thinking. Chatter and banter swirled around her.

She kept thinking that *something* was going to happen. Something would keep her from leaving. Fate would intervene. The flight would be cancelled; her ticket would prove unacceptable. Maybe Mark had hidden Spike in her purse or cosmetics case, and she'd be detained for that reason. *Something was going to happen.*

She had an appealing vision of a fleeing plane hijacker crashing into her. She saw herself falling, breaking a leg. She couldn't leave then! Mike, terrified for her safety, would sweep her up in his arms and beg her never to leave.

Yet nothing happened. No handy hijacker appeared. Her legs remained strong and unbroken. Mike showed no sign of being in a begging mood. She checked her larger suitcase and held on to the cosmetics case. She got a cup of coffee and saw her hand shake as she drank it. With relentless inevitability the numbers on her digital watch kept leaping forward.

She'd be on the plane in a few minutes, headed back to where she'd come from. Dull job, no Mike. He was going around shaking hands, telling everyone goodbye.

He seemed cheerful and happy, kidding around with everyone, telling the guys they'd all be in kilts next year. But when he got to Lynn, his expression changed. The smile vanished and his eyes turned somber.

"Well. The lady of the night."

An ambiguous statement, said in an equally ambiguous tone. They just looked at each other. His eyes were a blue enigma that told her nothing, and all his mouth said was "I don't suppose you've changed your mind about the job?"

That was it, she realized with a hollow despair. One line, faintly hostile. Nothing dramatic was going to happen to force her to stay; fate was not going to intervene. She was going home to her dull job, her ordinary apartment, her cardboard-cutout future.

And then a new and startling thought struck her.

Something would happen if she *made* it happen.

Carefully she squeezed all thoughts of Mike off in a shadowy corner of her mind. Leave Mike out of this, she told herself; consider only the job. That was a little like leaving the sunrise out of a morning, but she did the best she could.

As castle secretary she'd no longer be merely a tourist in Scotland; she'd have the opportunity to see and know the country as no tourist ever could. There'd be the excitement of meeting new people every week or two, people more cosmopolitan and interesting than she'd ever meet back at SunnyDay. She'd be living in a castle. The job could be a jumping-off point from which to find other jobs in even more exotic locales, a whole new and exciting life. It was suddenly like looking into a glossy bubble, all shimmery with wonderful possibilities.

Miss Prudence, however, immediately snatched up her needles and started jabbing at the bubble. The salary wasn't as shaky as it had been before Mike's computer game deal came through, but it didn't have SunnyDay's decades of secure reliability behind it. She *could* get stranded over here. Even if she got home safely she'd have to start all over on some new job, perhaps find she had to settle for lower-paying and even more boring work than the job at SunnyDay. And she'd have to find a new apartment to boot. Yes, working at the castle was definitely a risky proposition. Very insecure.

You want security? Tanya the Temptress challenged scornfully. *Go back and bury yourself at SunnyDay. Collect your pat on the back and your certificate of appreciation when you retire, when you'll still be ending letters, 'Have yourself a SunnyDay.'*

The phrase flew around inside Lynn's head like a mental vampire. If I have to type that phrase one more time, she thought wildly, I am going to stand on my desk and scream.

She looked out the window, where sunlight gleamed on a waiting plane. She weighed the balances of her future on an internal scale. Perhaps taking the castle job *would* mean she'd have to go home and start over at some time, but would that be such an earth-shaking disaster? What did she really have to lose?

The answer came quickly enough to make her clutch the cosmetics case as if it were a lifeline. Her heart. That was what she had to lose.

No. It was too late for that, she knew when she looked into Mike's eyes again. She'd been deceiving herself in refusing to call what she felt for him love. She'd already lost her heart.

She twisted her fingers around the handle on the cosmetics case, holding it between herself and Mike. *Make it happen,* that reckless part of her urged. *Take a chance. Send those fussy worries about job security and heartbreak possibilities home and stay here. Do it!*

There had been such a long silence between them that Lynn thought he might have forgotten what he'd said. "About that job—" she said a little breathlessly.

"Yes?" Did she detect a hopeful spark in the blue eyes?

"I've decided to accept it."

"Right now?" Beneath the mustache, his jaw dropped in astonishment.

"Right now."

"Can you do that?"

"A week is rather short notice, but I'm sure the woman who has been filling in for me at SunnyDay will be happy to take the job permanently." He was still just standing there looking at her as if he couldn't believe this, and a fresh doubt jolted her. "Unless it wasn't a serious offer?"

"Oh, yes, it was serious."

But if she'd expected wild shouts of joy and passionate embrace, that wasn't what she got. Mike tore off to retrieve her luggage while she stood there and shakily pondered the potential results of her rash decision.

That decision seemed even more rash when Mike returned a few minutes later shaking his head. His blond wig was slightly askew, but he didn't seem to notice. "It's too late. They'll try to intercept the suitcase in London, but I wouldn't count on it."

By that time the others had realized something strange was going on and questions flew at her from all directions. Lynn just shook her head and said she was staying, and then it was time to board the plane, and everyone was suddenly more concerned about themselves and going home than in Lynn.

Lynn and Mike stood at a window and watched the plane take off. In a few moments it was out of sight, disappearing into the blue sky as her little paper airplane had disappeared into the secret passageway. Except this plane was going somewhere, and maybe she should have been on it.

* * *

On the drive back to the castle Mike tossed the blond wig in the back seat. Seeing him halfway between personalities was distracting, but Lynn briskly stuck to the subject of her new responsibilities. The next guests were arriving Tuesday. The new cook, maids and other help would be trickling in on Sunday and Monday. Because time was so short, Lynn volunteered to help get the rooms in shape for the group of guests, after which she would assume her regular secretarial duties. Mike assigned her a smaller room in an area of employees' quarters near the kitchen. It was all very businesslike.

Lynn poked around in closets and drawers until she found some discarded old clothes, ill-fitting but clean, that she could use to work in. She cleaned bedrooms, thankful to find that Mark had taken Spike with him, had a sandwich for lunch and went back to cleaning.

She also wrote letters to her father, her sister, her mother and stepfather, telling each of them of her decision to work in Scotland for a while, trying to make it sound like a very casual and ordinary thing to do.

Then, after calculating that an evening telephone call from Scotland would reach the States during daytime hours, Lynn called Melody at the apartment. Melody was excited about Lynn's decision to stay, but she didn't seem as surprised as Lynn expected she would be. Her only regret was that Lynn wouldn't be around for her August wedding to Lance. They made arrangements about shipping Lynn's clothes and disposing of other miscellaneous items. Melody then asked about Lynn's car, and, after a long shaky moment, Lynn told her to sell that, too.

Lynn then called her SunnyDay boss at his home, apologizing for disturbing him on a Saturday. He seemed shocked by what she knew must appear to him a wildly out-of-character decision, but he wished her well and didn't complain about her short notice on leaving the job. She was not, she thought wryly, exactly indispensable at SunnyDay.

After she put the phone down, a jolt of panic hit her. Until then she could simply have changed her mind and taken another flight back to the States, but with these letters and calls she had cut all her ties to home and security. For better or worse, she was in Scotland. She had nothing but a scantily-equipped cosmetics case to her name, a job that was about as secure as a car with three months' payments past due and she was in love with a four-personality baron who was as unpredictable as the Scottish weather.

Suddenly it all seemed as colorfully implausible as some rock video. She, sensible, cautious Lynn Marquet, had done this? Miss Prudence, where are you? How did you let me get into this?

But Miss Prudence had gone into shock and was curled in a mental corner, no help at all.

Yet, in spite of the panic, Lynn also felt a certain exhilaration that surprised her. Because everything that panicked her was also marvelously exciting, a wonderful adventure. She was living in a castle! And she felt the strangest sense of freedom, as if she'd just discarded lead weights tied to her feet.

Recklessly, as she poked around in the cavernous kitchen to see what there was for dinner, she helped herself to champagne left over from the previous night's going-away celebration. It was still bubbly, and she had a second glass. By the time Mike strode into the kitchen a little later, her exhilaration was fizzy around the edges. She waved the glass at him in airy greeting.

"What're you doing?" he demanded.

"Fixing something to eat." She motioned toward the pans of Lily's leftovers heating on the stove.

"I meant with the champagne."

"I'm celebrating my new job." When he didn't say anything, she added with an impish tilt of head, "Don't you think that calls for a toast?"

She poured a glass of champagne for him. She felt giddy and reckless and the thought occurred to her that they were the only two people in the castle. A castle with ten bedrooms and not even Castle Cat for a chaperon. That thought, which at some more sensible moment might have made her feel apprehensive, instead glowed like a seductive flame at the end of a dark tunnel.

He took the glass of champagne and they clicked the rims together lightly. "To your new job," he said.

But instead of sipping from his glass he lifted it to her mouth. She offered hers to him, and they drank together, eyes locked. She saw the smolder of desire in his and knew her own reflected the same emotion. She hadn't taken the job solely because of all those reasons she'd given herself. She also had taken it because of him, because she loved him. The back of her hand rested lightly against his jaw.

"Perhaps you're sorry now that you offered me the job?" she asked softly, invitingly.

"It may have been a rash decision," he muttered.

It was not the answer she had expected. He stepped backward, as if he were wary of her. She slammed the glass on the counter so hard that the remaining champagne sloshed over the rim.

"Rash decision!" she sputtered. "You mentioned the job at least three times. I'd hardly call that rash."

"You're burning the food," he pointed out.

She whirled and grabbed a pan, but it was too late. The delicate sauce was already scorched on the bottom. She rescued what she could and they sat down to eat at the kitchen table.

"I'm glad I didn't hire you as the new cook," Mike said.

"Perhaps you should have offered my job to your midnight swimming companion, since you don't seem particularly delighted that I'm here," Lynn retorted in an equally unfriendly tone. She was suddenly aware of how she looked in her wardrobe of discards: shapeless shirt and baggy pants cinched at the waist with string, hair tied back with a stray piece of yarn. Not exactly the garb of the irresistible temptress.

He paused in the process of picking burned mushrooms out of the sauce. He didn't ask what she was referring to and merely snapped, "What were you doing, lurking in the bushes and spying?"

"I happened to glance out the window—"

"I couldn't sleep. I took a walk. A swim seemed like a good idea at the time, although it seemed a less good idea when I had uninvited company a little later. If you'd watched a minute or two longer, you'd have seen me tell her to get her clothes back on before she caught pneumonia. Crazy Americans," he added with a scowl and shake of head.

Look who's talking, Lynn thought, but she didn't say anything. She also thought about asking who his hot-blooded visitor had been, but she realized it really didn't matter.

"Perhaps I should apologize for what I was thinking, then," she said stiffly.

"Perhaps you should."

"Perhaps you also owe me an apology," she suggested.

"For what?"

"For saying I wasn't accepting the job because I was trying to force a marriage proposal out of you. Obviously that wasn't true, because I've accepted the job."

"That's the only reason you stayed? Because of the job?"

"Working in Scotland is an opportunity that doesn't come along every day," she pointed out, not exactly answering his question.

After they finished eating he went upstairs to collect the bundles of sheets she'd removed from the bedrooms, and she cleaned up the kitchen. He peered into the kitchen only long enough to say he was going over to the cottage and would see her in the morning.

Lynn's earlier fizzy mood had now gone flat as week-old champagne. She determinedly reminded herself of all those fabulous reasons she'd given herself for accepting this job.

But perhaps she had underestimated how painful being around him was going to be when he treated her exactly as what she was: an employee.

The new staff started arriving the following morning, and the next guests were going to be provided for in a manner considerably more befitting a castle with a baron host. The cook—the *chef*, as Lynn immediately thought of him—was in his sixties, silver-haired, elegant. He also liked cats, and Castle Cat found himself in a cat heaven of delightful tidbits.

The rooms in the employees' area of the castle filled up rapidly with housekeeper, maids, kitchen assistant and gardener. Lynn's suitcase came back from London, and she bought a few more things when she went in to Glasgow to pick it up. She assumed her office duties and immediately realized that Mike probably had been missing important phone calls about renting the castle. A suggestion the accountant had made was to lower the rate for stays longer than a week, and she was pleased to have a guest change a reservation from one to two weeks when she mentioned this on the phone. She always remembered to ask, when a reservation was made, specifically how many guests would be coming.

The new guests arrived by car from London, a wealthy older couple with three grandchildren, a nanny, a personal maid and their own chauffeur in tow. On the third day of their stay their divorced son, father of one of the grandchildren, arrived. He was a well-known British soccer player, handsome and dashing, presently recuperating from a knee injury. Lynn realized, when he was very friendly with her, that one of her thoughts about the potential of this job was quite valid: she was indeed meeting people she never would have met back at SunnyDay.

With the new guests, Mike was himself, a "working" baron who jumped in to help whenever help was needed. He might be found taking the children for a rowboat ride on the ond, trimming shrubbery or working on the castle car. He exhibited no abrupt switches of personality.

Yet Lynn knew the other parts were there. She saw a flash of superstud Tristan in his eyes when he encountered her taking a stroll with the soccer player. She suspected the possibility that she might succumb to another man's charms was more assault on Mike's ego than his heart. Money-conscious Barry was there when Mike went over bills with her, pointing out economies that must be made. A couple of times when they were working late at the cottage, she thought perhaps he had something other than work on his mind. Once she thought she felt his fingertips caress the back of her neck, but when she glanced around she decided it must have been an accidental touch.

By the time the first family of guests left, Lynn was torn between knowing that the job was everything she'd hoped and a feeling that she'd made the wrong decision in staying. The woman had told her if she ever decided she wanted to work in London, to look them up. The soccer-playing son had taken her to a fantastic dinner in Edinburgh one evening. The chef, who had cooked for several celebrities, had an endless supply of entertaining stories to tell about them.

Yet Lynn was always aware of a dull ache within her. She was in love with Mike. It was with her every minute of every day. When Mike was close, her skin tingled, as if she were in the vicinity of some high-voltage line. It made logical thought difficult. Yet when she wasn't close to him thoughts of him were equally distracting.

She enjoyed the job; she loved living in the old castle, too. Yet she was beginning to think that those joys were not compensation enough for the pain of being in love with a man who viewed her only as a competent secretary. Perhaps it would be better if she just went back to California. She was not going to get over Mike when she was around him every day.

The staff had two days off between the departure of the guests and arrival of the next group. Most of the other em-

ployees left the castle for that time, but Lynn didn't. She
planned to spend the first afternoon taking photos, with the
gloomy thought that perhaps she wouldn't be there much
longer.

The day turned out to be less than ideal for photo taking,
cool and misty, but she went ahead with her plans anyway.

She took photos of the castle from several angles, the now
nicely manicured grounds, the cottage, ham-actor Castle
Cat in various poses. She walked around the ponds, got
some nice shots of the picturesque cemetery, and of the
swans.

She left her small camera under a tree near the water while
she picked some flowers for her room. She didn't hear anyone approaching, and she whirled, startled, when a voice
spoke.

"Lynn, I want to talk to you."

Mike stood there, his decisive words hanging in the air.
He was wearing a dark business suit with the clan tartan tie
and looked every inch the dignified yet dashing baron. Apparently he'd just returned from a business meeting in
Edinburgh that he'd mentioned. His expression suggested
that either the meeting had not gone well or that he was unhappy with Lynn about something. Perhaps she wouldn't
have to quit; maybe he was going to fire her. Yet even as
apprehension surged through her, movement behind him
caught her attention.

One of the swans had come out of the water to inspect her
camera. He took a tentative peck at it.

She rushed by Mike, waving her arms indignantly. "Hey,
get away from there! Leave that alone!"

The swan flapped its wings at her unexpected charge. It
retreated toward the water, but it took the small camera with
it. Lynn stopped at the water's edge, astonished at the unlikely sight of her camera rapidly heading toward deep water in the bill of the swan. She'd paid one hundred and
nineteen dollars for that camera!

She plunged into the water after the swan. She was no match for its elegant speed, but the swan seemed to think this an interesting new game and circled around her as she foundered in frustration trying to catch up with it.

"Help me!" she yelled back at Mike.

Mike tore off his jacket and shoes and plunged in. With a few swift strokes he was beside her. "Don't panic. I'll save you!" He wrapped one arm around her. "Just relax and—"

"I'm not drowning!"

Mike let go and treaded water. "Then what the hell are you yelling help for?" Water plastered his hair to his forehead.

"I wanted you to help me catch your stupid swan and relieve my camera!"

"I jumped in the water in my best suit to save a *camera*?"

With a grim look he took off after the swan. Mike's determined chase apparently impressed the swan more than Lynn's efforts had. It flapped its wings in alarm and headed for the far shore. Lynn followed, slipping and sliding when she reached wading depth.

Mike was standing in ankle-deep water. "I think he dropped it around here somewhere," he said. He did not seem inclined to look for the camera. He took off his shirt and wrung a stream of water out of it.

Lynn finally spotted the camera. She reached for it, slipped, scrambled frantically with feet and hands to keep from falling and wound up flat on her belly in the water. To add insult to injury the swan came over and brazenly tried to snatch the camera back.

Mike shooed the swan away, stuck the camera in his pants pocket and hauled Lynn out of the water. He slung her over his bare shoulder as if she were a soggy piece of firewood and started around the pond with her.

She pounded his back with her fists. "What are you doing? Put me down!"

"You're shivering and turning blue. I'm going to get yo[u] warmed up before you catch something."

"I do not need warming up." She struggled more wildl[y] kicking and flinging her arms and throwing her weig[ht] around on his shoulder. "Put me down!"

Her struggles had an effect, but not the one she i[n]tended. She threw him off balance on the slippery edge [of] the pond, and they both went down. They landed half in th[e] water, half out of it.

Lynn raised up on one elbow and looked down at hi[m.] The lady of the night had done it once more, she realize[d] ruefully, and it wasn't even dark. She wiped a smear of mu[d] off his face.

"This really isn't working, is it?" she said. "I guess I['d] better go home...." Her words trailed off helplessly. He ha[d] dirt on his face, a stray white feather caught in his hair an[d] a tartan tie incongruously plastered to his bare chest. An[d] she loved him.

She started to get up, but he held her down with a har[d] arm around her waist.

"You're right. This isn't working. Not like this. You'[re] driving me crazy."

"I'm a good secretary," she said defensively, although sh[e] realized that might be irrelevant, considering what she'd ju[st] done to him.

"I don't give a damn about your secretarial abilities."

His hands held her shoulders hard against the ground an[d] his mouth descended to hers. His wet hair splattered her fac[e] with water. Their chilled lips met, and instantly they we[re] chilled no more. The warmth spread through Lynn, flus[h]ing her face, heating her body. She lost awareness of co[ld] water and slippery mud. Her arms went around him, palm[s] brushing the water from his shoulders. She kissed him back[,] lips and tongue saying all the things she'd been keeping [to] herself for days.

"That's why you're driving me crazy," he muttered whe[n] he finally lifted his head. "Because I keep wanting to d[o] that. And more. I was ready to stuff that soccer player and his smooth line into the secret passageway and nail it shut.''

He kissed her again, and she felt the heat of his body even through the layers of her wet clothing. Miss Prudence whispered cautions but Lynn paid no attention. Whatever was going to happen, she *wanted* it to happen. Whatever Mike was ready to give, she was ready to accept, even if it didn't fit with all her cautious ideas of how things should be. She savored the pepperminty taste of his kiss, the muscular hardness of his body, the joined throb of their heartbeats.

She drifted on a magic carpet of delight, senses shutting off messages about cold water or uncomfortable ground and replacing them with sensuous shimmers of pleasure in the feel of him. And then Mike flung her back to earth with his next words.

''So that's why I'm firing you as my secretary.''

''What?'' she gasped. The delight evaporated and her wet clothes suddenly felt frozen to her body.

''But there's another position open.''

''Oh?''

''This one is a lot more risky than your secretarial job. It doesn't have the security of a steady paycheck. The hours are long, and there are no days off.''

''What kind of work would this involve?'' she asked warily.

''A little of everything. Companion and confidante, friend and lover....''

Job description of a mistress. Miss Prudence gave a gasp of indignation, but Tanya the Temptress just said recklessly, *Go for it!* Lynn hit a middle-of-the-road answer when she said carefully, ''I might consider that.''

''Lynn, I love you. I started falling in love with you the minute I first saw you. I've fallen more in love every minute since then.''

''And stayed so far away from me that you couldn't touch me with the proverbial ten-foot pole.''

He laughed ruefully and kissed away a drop of water clinging to her eyelashes. "Because I knew that if we made love I'd never be able to let you go. I'd be committed, heart, body and soul. And part of me wanted that, and another part didn't."

Lynn didn't have to ask which part of him had temper tantrums against commitment.

"But I've wasted enough time letting old Tristan and his doubts keep me from doing what I want to do. I've battled him to a standstill in our arguments over commitment."

"Mike, just what is this position you're offering?"

"I think the official title would be baroness."

"You're asking me to marry you?"

"I realize this isn't the most romantic of moments for a marriage proposal, but, yes, I'm asking you to marry me."

Lynn desperately wanted to fling all caution aside, to take him at his word and accept what he offered, but his accusation that she'd tried to force a marriage proposal out of him hung over her like the mist above the pond.

"Maybe all you really want is a lover." She caressed one eyebrow with a fingertip, and a drop of water trickled down his temple. "And perhaps someday you'd be sorry you offered more than that."

"Lynn, I'm lying in cold water and mud, half undressed. I've ruined my suit. I don't want to point an accusing finger, but I do believe you put me here. All of this is not conducive to a wildly amorous mood. Could a man ask a woman to marry him under these conditions if he didn't love her enough to want a forever commitment? The lady of the night made her biggest strike right square on my heart."

Lynn lifted a handful of pond water and dribbled it onto his bare back, the small equivalent of a cold shower. "Still love me?"

He shivered when the cold water hit his skin, but he didn't waver. "Yes. I love you."

"Who knows what other disasters I may cause?"

"I'll take my chances. If you'll take a chance on me." His voice turned husky with seriousness. "Because, as you once pointed out, marrying me isn't exactly stepping into solid security. The computer deal could turn out to be a bust. We might lose the castle. And with it goes the baroness title. You might wind up with nothing but me."

Nothing but him. Which was all she really wanted. None of the rest of it mattered to her. And yet . . .

"Earlier you said you wanted to talk to me. About what?"

"The same things we're talking about now."

"What if I'd gone home?"

"I was still battling Tristan then. But I'd have come after you, because I wouldn't let his doubts cost me you." He tilted his head as if listening to some inner voice. He smiled. "I don't hear a thing now. I think Tristan is gone for good. No more foolish multiple personalities, just you and me."

He got to his feet and pulled Lynn up beside him. "Look, I know I'm a risky proposition. You pointed that out to me. But one thing is as secure and solid as that old castle." He kissed her lightly, sweetly on the mouth. "My love. There appears to be just one problem."

"Problem?"

"You haven't given me an answer yet."

Lynn reached up and put her arms around him and kissed him. "I love you," she said simply.

"Then all we have to do is figure out how we go about getting married in Scotland and do it. *Now.*"

"I think I'd like to change clothes first."

"If you insist."

"There's just one thing." She drew a swirl in the damp mat of his chest hair. "I hope Tristan hasn't *completely* disappeared. . . ."

"Why in the world would you want old Tristan around?"

"Oh, he has his good points," she murmured, remembering one silent, scorching kiss. People who had only one personality must lead very dull, predictable lives. "I'll bet he has some terrific ideas...."

Mike grinned. "Could be."

Tanya the Temptress peeked out and she, too, had some interesting ideas. Lynn looked at the castle. "I want to make love in every room in the castle," she said dreamily.

Mike's blue eyes held a wicked gleam that definitely hinted at Tristan origins. "Okay, that takes care of our wedding night. Then what?"

Lynn slipped an arm around his waist, her imagination roving with reckless abandon through all the places she usually made it detour. "I imagine we'll think of something."

* * * * *

COMING NEXT MONTH

#718 SECOND TIME LUCKY—Victoria Glenn
A Diamond Jubilee Book!
Ailing Aunt Lizbeth glowed with health after Miles Crane kissed
her man-shy goddaughter Lara MacEuan. If Miles had his way,
his frail aunt would be on a rapid road to recovery!

#719 THE NESTING INSTINCT—Elizabeth August
Zeke Wilson's cynical view of love had him propose a marriage of
convenience to Meg Delany. Could his in-name-only bride
conceal her longing for a marriage of love?

#720 MOUNTAIN LAUREL—Donna Clayton
Laurel Morgan went to the mountains for rest and
relaxation...but Ranger Michael Walker knew fair game when
he saw it! The hunt was on, but who was chasing whom?

#721 SASSAFRAS STREET—Susan Kalmes
Callie Baker was furious when the man who outbid her at an
antique auction turned out to be Nick Logan, her new boss. Nick,
on the other hand, was thrilled....

#722 IN THE FAMILY WAY—Melodie Adams
Fiercely independent divorcée Sarah Jordan was quite in the
family way—and had no plans for marriage. But smitten Steven
Carlisle had plans of his own—to change her mind!

#723 THAT SOUTHERN TOUCH—Stella Bagwell
Workaholic Whitney Drake ran from her fast-paced New York
life to the Louisiana bayou—and right into the arms of Caleb
Jones. But could his loving touch convince her to stay forever?

AVAILABLE THIS MONTH:

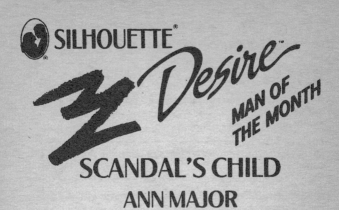

You'll flip . . . your pages won't!
Read paperbacks *hands-free* with

Book Mate · I

The perfect "mate" for all your romance paperbacks

Traveling • Vacationing • At Work • In Bed • Studying
• Cooking • Eating

Perfect size for all standard paperbacks, this wonderful invention makes reading a pure pleasure! Ingenious design holds paperback books OPEN and FLAT so even wind can't ruffle pages — leaves your hands free to do other things. Reinforced, wipe-clean vinyl-covered holder flexes to let you turn pages without undoing the strap . . . supports paperbacks so well, they have the strength of hardcovers!

Pages turn WITHOUT opening the strap

SEE-THROUGH STRAP

Reinforced back stays flat

Built in bookmark

BOOK MARK

BACK COVER HOLDING STRIP

10 x 7¼ opened
Snaps closed for easy carrying, too

DIAMOND JUBILEE
CELEBRATION!

It's Silhouette Books' tenth anniversary, and what better way to celebrate than to toast *you*, our readers, for making it all possible. Each month in 1990, we'll present you with a DIAMOND JUBILEE Silhouette Romance written by an all-time favorite author!

Welcome the new year with *Ethan*—a LONG, TALL TEXANS book by Diana Palmer. February brings Brittany Young's *The Ambassador's Daughter*. Look for *Never on Sundae* by Rita Rainville in March, and in April you'll find *Harvey's Missing* by Peggy Webb. Victoria Glenn, Lucy Gordon, Annette Broadrick, Dixie Browning and many more have special gifts of love waiting for you with their DIAMOND JUBILEE Romances.

Be sure to look for the distinctive DIAMOND JUBILEE emblem, and share in Silhouette's celebration. Saying thanks has never been so romantic....